below deck

below deck

sophie hardcastle

ALLEN&UNWIN

First published in Australia and New Zealand in 2020 by Allen & Unwin

First published in Great Britain in 2020 by Allen & Unwin, an imprint of Atlantic Books Ltd

Allen & Unwin, an imprint of Atlantic Books Ltd
Ormond House
26–27 Boswell Street
London WC1N 3JZ

Phone: 020 7269 1610
Fax: 020 7430 0916
E-mail: UK@allenandunwin.com
Web: www.allenandunwin.com/uk

A CIP catalogue record for this book is available from the British Library.

Hardback ISBN: 978 1 91163 052 4
E-Book ISBN: 978 1 76087 230 4

Printed in Great Britain by TJ International Ltd, Padstow, Cornwall

10 9 8 7 6 5 4 3 2 1

For Robbie

dark pink

'You dying in your twenties is not romantic,' he told me, his eyes dense black, half in shadow. He shook his head. 'It would be a waste.'

I remember that we were in my living room at the time, and that I didn't say anything back, but I thought about it for a long time after, the word *waste* swirling like an oil slick. I knew he was right. It would be a waste. But when I'd said I would die in my twenties, it was never about the romance of it, the old story of the young artist perishing before her time. It was more of a knowing. A knowing that it was my time.

I die on the eve of the day I was born, twenty-nine, almost thirty. I've always liked the numbers twenty-nine, two and nine, much more than I've ever liked thirty, three and zero: two is red, and nine dark pink; three is uneasy green and zero is empty white. But contrary to what you might be thinking, I don't do it on purpose. Not really.

Then again, maybe I do. We're made up of myriad choices, aren't we?

I shrug. Shiver. It's cold here, on the wet stern deck, on the edge of this decade and the next. Beneath me, it is dark, icebergs suspended in the grey. It is all spreading. And I look across at Brooke and she winks and I smile and it hurts my face.

I hold my breath. Do we choose to breathe?

I don't know. I still don't know. I wish you'd told me the answer. I wish you'd told me a lot of things.

Like that when I finally see the green flash, it will be equally amazing and dull.

Or that life is a series of words and the punctuation is in all the wrong places and when you want to take a breath someone has removed the comma so you, have to take one there and if you didn't too bad it's already, gone.

Maggie, I wish you'd told me. At sea, no one can hear you scream.

sea garden

sea rose

Caught in the in-between, I imagine the earth is rocking. It's all back and forth, back and forth.

But now I'm coming to, and there's drool caked to my chin and fur on my teeth, and I'm peeling apart puffy eyelids to see the sun through a skylight that's only a few feet above my head. The sun is swinging back and forth in the sky and I realise the earth really is rocking. I prop myself up on one elbow. My head is pounding like someone's clobbered me with a brick. I look around and, as the room comes into focus, I wait for this all to make sense. But it doesn't. The walls are curved, and no wider than the bed—if you'd even call this a bed. I'm lying on a wafer-thin mattress, wedged between a huge canvas bag and a fishing rod. There's a weird thumping outside and, when I look up, the sun is still swinging. I feel a tightening in my chest, a fierce contraction of my ribcage, like my breath is caught and can't get out. Where the fuck *am* I?

I'm wearing clothes, at least: a silk dress, my denim jacket, two pink socks and one boot. I feel under my dress and I've got undies on. The contents of my bag are sprawled around my pillow. Wallet, check. Cards and cash are still there. I grab my phone, hands trembling. The battery is dead. 'Shit,' I mutter.

Wriggling out of the bed, I find my other boot on the floor beside a bucket full of sponges. My legs are wobbling as I clamber out of the room. I knock my head on the roof. Who the hell designed this house? I'm tall but I'm not *that* tall.

The earth is still rocking as I stumble into a room with a kitchenette, sling bunk beds, slit windows, and a table that's bolted to the floor. I feel my way through, grabbing corners and edges for balance, to keep myself upright, dragging myself towards a ladder that leads to open sky.

Climbing up, it takes my eyes a second to adjust. The light is piercing.

'Oh. My. God.' The words are barely a whisper.

In front of me is an old man wearing an oilskin jacket, an orange beanie. His skin is weathered, salt-encrusted, with sunspots and a coarse white beard. Beyond him is ocean. Its surface is dark and choppy. My body shudders, my spine curls. The horizon is impossibly far away.

'Morning.'

I stare at him blankly.

He laughs.

'Where am I?'

'Sorry?' he says. 'You'll have to speak up.' He puts a finger to his ear. 'Bit deaf.'

'Where am I?' I repeat, louder this time.

'You're on the Tasman.'

At my feet, there are ropes coiled around metal stumps, and lines threaded up a towering pole. The old man pulls on one of the ropes and the creases in the sail above me are smoothed out, like skin pulled tight around bone. I feel the boat pucker, then lift a little.

'The *what*?'

'The Tasman Sea,' he says, pointing to the endless expanse of ocean, as if I'm meant to recognise *this* water as distinct from any *other* water. 'But more specifically,' the old man says, 'you're on a yacht.' He rests a hand on the boat's deck. 'And her name is *Sea Rose*.'

I feel like a hand is wrapped around my throat, squeezing. I might throw up. 'I need to get off.'

'You will. In a few days . . . when we get to New Zealand.'

The blood drains from my face. 'What?!'

'I'm sailing her to New Zealand and needed an extra hand. You said you wanted to come.'

'Are you kidding? When did I say that?'

'Last night.'

I sink back into alcohol-soaked hours, searching for something, *anything*. But last night is a gaping black hole.

'Why would you let me agree to this? I was legless last night!'

The boat rises over a wave, slams down. My head hurts. I feel bile surge in the back of my throat. 'You're basically kidnapping me.'

'I'm what?'

'Kidnapping me! You'll go to jail for this.'

'Well,' he says, reclining with a wide smile, 'I'll only go to jail if someone finds out . . . I guess I'll just have to kill you.'

I take half a step away and my ankle rolls on a coil of rope. I fall back, landing heavily on the deck, the wind knocked out of my lungs.

Suddenly, the old man bursts into laughter, his eyes disappearing between deep wrinkles. Between bouts he wheezes, 'You right, kid?'

I try to speak. But I can't.

'Look over your shoulder,' he says.

I clamber to my feet and turn around to see land. A stretch of beach, houses dotted between greenery, a rocky headland, a lighthouse . . . I know that lighthouse. It's Barrenjoey. Sydney. We're still in Sydney.

I turn back to him.

'You know where we are now?'

I nod.

'We're going to the RPA Yacht Club in Newport; I need to drop my *Rose* off for a clean. Should be there within the hour with this wind. I'm giving you a lift back to the city.'

'Chivalry, now . . . doesn't change . . .' I cough; I'm still winded from the fall. 'You . . . kidnapped me.'

'You, young lady, were blind. Couldn't even tell me your name. Was I supposed to let you go home like that? No. Jane and I had to carry you to the boat.'

'Who's Jane?'

'She manages the restaurant at the CYC. Apparently she found you in the women's bathroom. I let you sleep the night on board . . . Woke you up this morning, said I needed to get going and you told me to leave you be.'

'Well, I don't remember that.' The cold wind is snaking around my body. I cross my arms, trying to summon any recollection of the night before. 'Where did *you* sleep?'

He meets my eye. 'In my bed,' he says. 'At my house.' And there's something in his deadpan delivery, in the steadiness of it, that makes me believe him. He smiles gently. 'You don't need to worry about me, kid—I've only ever loved one woman.' The smile fades and he looks beyond the horizon. 'And she's gone now.'

I relax my arms. 'What was her name?'

He rests his hand on the boat's deck again, smooths it the way you touch a lover. 'Robynne. Robynne Rose.' He clears his throat. 'Anyway, I didn't mean to kidnap you, but I gotta be at the boatyard by ten, and assumed you'd be out until we got there.'

Relief washes over me. 'This is so weird,' I say, shuffling towards him, my arm outstretched, offering my hand. 'But whatever . . . My name's Olivia.'

He gives me his callused, leather hand and we shake. 'Mac.'

At first glance, Mac is grey slate. Cool and hard. But then he laughs and the slate ripples. I see then that he is impossibly deep, like dark ocean. Inky stories twist in him like sea serpents in underwater caves.

On the rare occasions when my dad told stories, they were painfully obvious. Like etching words into sleek metal with a needle, he'd trace them over and over until they bled.

Mac is different. His way is guiding me through crevasses studded with barnacles and adorned with starfish. Alive with dancing weeds.

Instantly, he reminds me of my pa who could tell stories that filled any room with colour.

Mac tells me about a time he and Robynne got so drunk on rum on a beach in Barbados that they rowed back to the wrong boat and made love in someone else's cockpit. I lean in. His voice is like thunder beneath a roll cloud, bold and exciting. Electric. I could listen to him for hours.

He pauses. 'You cold?'

I shake my head. 'Nah, this tea is fixing me up.'

He smiles. 'Good.'

I'm sitting with Mac in the cockpit, wearing one of his wet-weather jackets. It's huge, creasing and folding around me as I lift my hands to take a sip of tea. 'Thank you.'

'You're welcome.'

I look past Mac's shoulder. The surface of the sea is raised like pricked skin, a wash of goosebumps as autumn reaches out into winter.

'How old are you?' he asks.

'You aren't meant to ask a woman her age.'

He snorts. 'You, kid, are not a woman.'

'Excuse me?'

'Not yet, anyway.' He draws the wheel closer to him and the boat tips harder on its side. 'Are you even old enough to drink?'

'I'm twenty-one,' I say. Two, red. One, pale yellow. 'I can even drink in America.'

He rolls his eyes, a wry smile bending his lips. 'How's your head?'

'Sore.'

Mac laughs. 'I bet. You could barely stand last night.'

I feel the hairs raise at the nape of my neck. 'Don't . . . I don't want to know.'

'You're right,' he concedes. 'I'm sorry. Didn't look like it was your fault anyway.'

I tilt my head. 'What?'

'That boy you were with—he looked like a right piece of work.'

And just like that, the previous evening washes over me like a wave across the deck.

Dinner at the Cruising Yacht Club on Sydney Harbour. And Adam. Clean-shaven, Rolex-wearing, Adam.

'He's my boyfriend.'

'He left you passed out in the bathroom.'

'We were having an argument.' Though perhaps what I really mean is that Adam was having an argument with Adam. And I was both between and outside. Silent. Strangled.

'An argument about what?'

'My . . . my career, I guess. We're just about to finish our economics degrees; I've been offered an internship at Lazard, this big investment bank, but I told him I don't know if I'm going to take it,' I explain. And I'm so ready for the usual response—*What an opportunity!*—that at first I don't hear what Mac actually says.

'Sorry,' I say. 'What was that?'

'I said, what's it got to do with him?'

'Well, he said I was throwing away a once-in-a-lifetime opportunity,' I say, skimming over: *I know ten guys who would kill for that gig.* Skimming over: *You're lucky they even gave it to you.*

Lucky, I think. After all that work.

Sheer luck. A fluke.

Mac shakes his head, and then, with a certainty that sets my world on fire, he says, 'You're your own person, Oli. Maybe he's scared of that.'

I laugh. 'No one's ever called me that before.'

'Oli?'

'Yeah.'

'Do you like it?'

I smile. 'Yeah, I do.'

We watch from the restaurant at the yacht club as the *Sea Rose* is hoisted from the water and slung up in the shipyard. Mac has bought me a huge strawberry milkshake and a portion of chips. I mix mayonnaise and tomato sauce together on a plate until it's salmon pink, flecked with pepper, and Mac says, 'Your accent—you didn't grow up here, did you?'

I shake my head. 'Lived in Manly until I was five, then Hong Kong and Singapore.' I slurp my milkshake.

'So what brought that about? Parents' work?'

'My dad heads the South-East Asia division of an oil company.'

'Oil, hey?'

'Yep.'

Mac opens his mouth to speak, then seems to change his mind. He looks over to the shipyard where the *Sea Rose* is cradled above the ground.

'I live with my grandpa in Manly now,' I explain. 'My dad sent me back here for uni.'

He turns back to me. 'The business degree?'

'Economics.'

'So what are you going to do now?'

'Dunno. Lazard, I guess . . .'

Mac gives me a sharp look. 'I thought you didn't want the internship?'

'Well, if it was up to me I would have studied art, but Dad said he wouldn't pay for that.'

Silence drapes between us.

I sigh. 'There's no money in art anyway.'

Mac laughs. 'You should meet this friend of mine.'

'Who?'

'Maggie.' His mouth wraps around her name with the same kindness as an arm around a friend's shoulder. 'She was a curator in London for years. Retired now. Lives here in Sydney with me.'

I edge forwards in my chair. 'That's cool.'

'You'll like her,' Mac assures me. 'She's an incredible woman.'

'When can I meet her?'

'I'm coming back up here on Wednesday to sail the *Sea Rose* back down to the CYC. Maggie's coming with me. How about you join us?'

I think of our sail into Pittwater this morning, how hard I'd laughed. I grin. 'Yeah, sure. I'd love to.'

'But no drinking Tuesday night, okay, kid?'

'Never again,' I say, my cheeks hot.

'Ha! Heard that before.' He helps himself to the last of my chips. 'Come on, let's get out of here.'

We're strolling across the car park, the sun falling through a hole in the clouds, when Mac excuses himself, tells me he'll be just a minute, and heads over to the shipyard. He walks up to the *Sea Rose*, touches his palm to the bottom of the boat. It is full and round, white with tendrils of brown algae. Mac whispers something as he smooths the fibreglass, kisses it softly. And I find myself feeling awkward suddenly, shifting my weight from one leg to another, like I'm spying on lovers, witnessing a moment reserved for someone else.

In the car, Mac turns on the radio.

I feel it coursing through me in a stream of soft reds. 'I love this song,' I say. 'It feels very pink.'

'Pardon me?'

'I said, it feels very pink.' Then, considering how odd that must sound, I laugh sheepishly. 'I don't know. It's just a feeling I have.'

Mac shakes his head. He's smiling. 'I can't wait for you to meet Maggie.'

sea lavender

When I can't find my keys, I empty my handbag on Pa's doormat. WELCOME TO PARADISE.

On my knees, I sift through the mess. 'Shit,' I mutter, standing to knock on the door. There's nothing Pa hates more.

I remember when I arrived here four years ago, jet-lagged and clammy with sweat, my entire life slung around my shoulders. How there'd been no answer to my knock at the door, though I could hear the TV blaring. How I'd called out, 'Hello?'

'WHAT?!'

His shout had been a shock of lime green.

Once there'd have been Nan, soft like a peach, opening the door, petals unfurling. Once there'd have been tea brewing and a tray of biscuits in the oven. Once there'd have been Pa's loving embrace, picking me up, swirling me around. Nan's smiling eyes and cheerful banter. Pa's wild stories and raucous laugh.

How jarring it was, that *WHAT.*

'It's Olivia,' I called.

'WHO?' he yelled over the blasting TV.

I thumped the door with my fist. 'Olivia!'

There were clumsy footsteps, and then the door cracked open. 'I'm not interested. Piss off.'

I grabbed hold of the door before he had a chance to close it. 'Pa, stop. It's me—it's Olivia.'

And then the door opened, and a man with skin more grey than the last time I'd seen it looked me up and down. He was wearing a cricket cap, an ironed white shirt, beige trousers and leather shoes. 'I thought you weren't coming till this afternoon,' he said.

I looked at my watch. 'It's three o'clock.'

Pa shrugged and stepped back, allowing me in. 'Looks heavy,' he said, gesturing to my rucksack. 'I'd help you but my back is screwed.' He rubbed his hip.

'No worries,' I said, following him in. He moved painfully slowly.

'Here's the lounge room,' he said, as if I'd never been here before. 'Kitchen.' Pointing to the cramped kitchen with lino floors, an empty fruit bowl. 'The balcony is best in the morning.'

I looked out to the balcony where a succulent sat shrivelled in a terracotta pot. 'I thought the point of owning a succulent was that it won't die,' I said.

Pa laughed, but the sound was shallow water. 'Everything dies.' He tapped a closed door. 'That's my room. When I'm in there, I'm not to be disturbed. Got it?'

I nodded.

Then he showed me the bathroom and the room that would be mine—instructing me not to touch the boxes under the desk or the box in the bottom of the cupboard—then excused himself to get back to the cricket.

I unpacked then returned to the living room, was ignored when I asked him if he wanted a cup of tea.

It wasn't till an ad came on the TV that Pa turned to me. 'Sorry I couldn't meet you at the airport. I've been busy.'

I looked around, taking in the half-completed crossword on the coffee table, the cricket resuming on the screen, the three empty beer bottles. 'All good,' I said. 'I like your hat.' But his attention was back on the cricket. He reached under the coffee table, grabbed a pack of cigarettes and lit one. That was new.

I stood in the kitchen, watching him suck on it, the embers burning. He exhaled, and a cloud filled the room. He cleared phlegm in his throat. His hands shook. I looked at his fingers, thin and knobbly, his nails yellowing, his wedding band loose. Even then I could see he was starving without her. Time eroding his body. But not fast enough.

The kettle on the stove began to whistle. I poured water over my tea, watched the water change colour, change shape. On the kitchen bench was a bouquet of lavender, brown stalks, the flowers limp and furry. I could only guess how long they'd been there.

When I visited as a child, Nan would hide lavender in my drawers, so that I'd carry the scent of her wherever I went. How magic it had seemed. But these were flowers dying as slowly as he was.

I joined Pa in the living room, and looked out and up the hill to where the lights on St Patrick's Seminary were coming on. 'Do you remember how you used to tell me there were fairies living in St Pat's, and that's why it lights up at night?' I asked, standing over him.

Pa shook his head. 'Can't imagine why I would have said something like that.'

I took the seat beside him. And so began four years of Pa's body tensing every time I sat in Nan's chair.

Now, the TV is blaring behind the door as usual, only I can hear there's a soap opera on. Pa never watches soap operas. He must be in a mood.

I brace myself, and knock.

There's no answer.

I knock louder.

Still nothing.

I call out. Knock again. Shout through the door.

'For fuck's sake,' I mutter. It's the third time I've locked myself out this month. He's ignoring me on purpose, I'm sure of it.

The door on the opposite side of the landing opens and Will sticks his head out. 'Locked out?' he says.

'Unfortunately yes.'

'You need a lanyard.'

I roll my eyes. 'Does your mum still have the spare key?'

'Unfortunately yes.'

'Very funny,' I say. He ducks back inside and returns a moment later with the key, chucks it to me.

'Nice catch.'

'Nice throw.'

He winks, says, 'See ya,' and goes back inside his apartment.

I let myself in. 'Hey,' I say as I pass Pa, who's sitting in his chair in the living room.

He ignores me.

In my room, I dump my bag on my bed, kick off my boots, shake off my jacket, walk back out and put the kettle on.

'Sorry I didn't come home last night, but you won't believe what happened to me.'

Silence. Not even a grunt to feign interest.

'Pa?' I say.

The kettle starts to whistle.

He must be really mad. Though I've stayed at Adam's before without telling him, so I'm not sure what the big deal is.

'Pa?' I say again, reaching for the kettle. I pull it off the stove, start to pour, though I'm not looking at the cup; I'm looking at my grandfather, slouched in front of the TV.

Boiling water dribbles over the bench, splashes my feet through my socks. I jump back. 'Ow, shit!'

He doesn't tell me off for swearing.

'Pa?' I whisper, rounding the bench. That strange slouch . . . I shiver and edge forwards.

His head is cocked oddly to one side, his neck folded.

I take another step.

And then I see them, his eyes, glazed, half open, milky. I reach forwards, my hand shaking, touch my fingertip to his cheek. It's warm. That means he's still alive, doesn't it?

'Pa!' I shout.

Will opens his door, laughing. 'How have you locked yourself—' He pauses, frowns. 'Are you okay?'

'N-no,' I stutter. 'There's something wrong with my pa.'

'Mum!' Will calls over his shoulder.

'What?' she sings out from the other room.

'*Mum!*'

'What is it? I'm busy!'

'*MUM!*' shouts Will.

Annie emerges a moment later.

'I think my pa's having a stroke,' I tell her.

'Oh, Christ,' Annie says, rushing past me. 'Will, call an ambulance.'

I follow her into my grandfather's apartment. She touches him. Shudders.

Outside, the lights on St Pat's come on, gold against dusk.

Annie takes his wrist, checks for a pulse. She exhales into the blue space where he doesn't.

'Honey, I'm so, so sorry,' she says.

'But he's warm. I felt him.'

Will comes in behind me. 'The ambulance is on its way.'

Annie shakes her head.

And suddenly, I feel myself touch the ground. Like I've spent my whole life floating around in outer space, and I'm just now feeling gravity for the first time. It's a shock, this force on my body.

The weight of it is crushing.

sea blossom

I sleep on Will's sofa, though it's not really sleeping. It's more of a waiting. Waiting for what? The hours grate against my skin. I'm not sad, though; at least, I don't think I am. I haven't cried.

Will told me I could. While we were brushing our teeth, he said, 'You can cry, you know.'

'I know,' I said, toothpaste frothing at the corners of my mouth. But I didn't.

All I feel is the density of my bones, the incredible weight of them.

Lying on the sofa, I watch the night turn into white. Annie gets up early for a swim. I close my eyes and listen to her sneak past me, treading lightly.

By the time she gets back, I've watched pink uncurl into blue.

'How'd you sleep?' she asks.

'Okay,' I lie.

'Have you heard back from your parents?'

'Got an email from my dad. They've booked flights. They'll be here on Tuesday.'

'Tomorrow?'

'No, next Tuesday.'

Annie stares at me blankly, uncomprehending.

'My dad has a big conference this weekend,' I explain.

'I thought your mum would want to come sooner. He was her dad, wasn't he?'

I shake my head. 'No. Dad's dad. Mum's parents both died before I was born.'

'I see . . . Still, I would have thought she'd want to come out sooner.'

'Dad would want her to fly with him,' I say.

'Right,' she says, but she looks troubled. Then she promises she'll help me in any way she can, tells me I'm welcome to sleep on their sofa for as long as I want.

I walk into the apartment and find it's not the sunken impression of Pa in his armchair that makes my skin crawl; it's the silence, the awful green of it, all muddy and murky.

I turn the TV on, turn it up loud, and let the sound of a woman chatting about a vacuum cleaner colour the room apricot. Outside, the sky is stretching blue. I walk into my bedroom and gaze out the window, across the pines that line the beach, beyond them, to the sea. It's spread like pleated fabric; swells lined one after another all the way to the horizon. That's what I missed most about Australia: the way the sky rests so evenly on the sea. An endless expanse of sky brought to a close. No smog, no pink grey. Just a fine, perfect line.

Hearing a cough behind me, I jump.

'Oh shit, sorry,' Will says. 'I didn't mean to scare you.'

He's standing in the doorway in track pants and a t-shirt.

'Aren't you meant to be at school?' I ask.

'Mum said I could have the day off.'

'What? Because you saw a dead person?'

Will looks away from me. He shrugs.

'That's nice of her.'

'I thought we could hang out.'

'Sure.'

'Only if you want to. But if you want to be alone . . .'

'No, no. It's fine. It'd be nice to have company . . .' I say. 'Wanna look through some dead person stuff?'

Will's eyes widen. 'That's messed up,' he says. 'But okay. Think I'll fit his clothes?'

'That's even worse!' I say.

We stare at each other a moment, then both burst into laughter. The hurt of it feels good; a cracking open of the chest that lets the heat out and the cold in. Like the bite of winter, the way it wakes you up.

Will comes into my room and flops down on my bed, watching me as I finally open the boxes under the desk and in the bottom of the cupboard. I've spent four years wondering what was inside them, but figured that while I lived in his house, I should respect Pa's wishes. In a way, it was better *not* to know what was in them—it was more fun to guess. I've always found a thrill in the darkness of the unknown.

It turns out my fantasies of gemstones and black pearls are wide of the mark. The boxes under the desk contain cookbooks and tablecloths. I fare better with the box at the bottom of the cupboard; to my delight, it's full of Nan's make-up. There are tubes of lipstick in every shade, bottles of perfume with yellowed labels, powder compacts, and nail polish in varying shades of red. I rummage through the lipsticks, eventually settling on a deep cherry. I smooth it across my lips, blow Will a kiss.

He laughs. 'What colour would suit me?'

'Hmm,' I say. 'We need something to make your eyes pop.' I find a hot pink. 'Perfect.'

Will puckers his lips.

'Hold still,' I say, as I colour them in. 'Aw, pretty!'

'I look gorge,' he says, pouting at his reflection in the mirror on my desk.

'We need outfits,' I say.

Pa's room is smaller than I remember, barely wider than the bed. Stepping into the room, I realise I probably haven't set foot in here since I was a kid climbing into bed between Nan and Pa on Christmas morning. How big the room had seemed then. How warm and wide the bed had felt. Pa might have died in his chair but, really, his life ended years ago. His life ended with hers.

I open the cupboard, and we're engulfed by the scent of stale tobacco.

'Are you okay?'

'Yeah,' I say. 'Are you?'

'It's just kind of weird, isn't it? How these were clothes that belonged to someone, and now they're just, I dunno . . .'

'Clothes.'

'Yeah.'

I shrug.

'Ooh, I like this,' Will says, picking out a tweed coat. He wriggles his lanky limbs into it.

'Suits you,' I say. I pull out a navy blazer. 'How about this for me?'

He nods. 'Strong vibes.'

I complete my outfit with suit pants, bright red socks and a pair of Nan's boots, which are embroidered with gold blossoms. Will wears a pair of emerald green cords, striped socks and suave leather shoes. He finishes off his outfit with a necklace of rose-pink pearls.

'We look expensive.'

Will laughs. 'We *are* expensive.'

'I should probably sort the rest out,' I say, contemplating aloud.

'Yeah, may as well. You'll have to sooner or later.'

'Can you please get me some garbage bags from the kitchen? They're in the third drawer down.'

'Sure,' he says, disappearing for a moment, returning with a handful of bags. 'Here.' He passes me one.

'Thanks,' I say as I pull a jacket off its coathanger. 'Keep anything you want . . . It'll all be going to charity.'

Will offers me a quiet smile and begins to help.

Once all the clothes have been sorted—save a few pieces for our own closets—we move on to the drawers in the bedside table.

'Oh my God!' Will exclaims. 'Look at these!' He pulls from the drawer a pack of playing cards, each with a photo of a different naked woman printed on the back. The pictures are highly saturated, giving the women brightly coloured nipples and shocks of pubic hair.

'Dirty dog,' Will says, shuffling through them. He looks up at me. 'Have you had sex?'

'Wow,' I say. 'That's, like, completely inappropriate.'

'Ha, sorry. Mum says I need a filter.'

'I reckon.'

'So have you?'

'What?'

'Had sex.'

'What's it to you?' I say coldly, but I can feel heat blooming on my cheeks.

Will shrugs. 'I have.'

'Me too. Kind of.'

'How do you kind of have sex?'

'Well, I mean, I've done it, but I haven't, you know, orgasmed. At least I don't think I have.'

'I think you'd know it if you did.'

'Okay then. I guess I haven't.'

'I never imagined Adam as a generous lover.'

'Hey,' I say, 'you're walking a very fine line.'

'Sorry,' he says, though he doesn't look it. 'Where is Adam, anyway?'

I shrug.

'I mean, why isn't he here?' Will persists.

'I haven't told him what happened yet.'

Will frowns. 'Why not?'

'We had a fight the other night.'

'So? You should still tell him.'

'I know. I'm going to.'

'Now?'

The thought of speaking to Adam right now is making my pulse quicken, every beat painful, so I change the subject. 'Right *now* I feel like getting out of here. How about we go drop these bags off?'

'Sure,' says Will. 'But I still think you should call him.'

'Later,' I say. 'Promise.'

We wear our outfits down the hill into Manly, where we leave the bags of clothes at an op shop. On the way home, we pass a gelato stand. I pull on Will's arm to stop him in front of it.

'I don't have any money,' he says.

'I do,' I tell him, eyeing off the flavours. Addressing the man tending the stand, I say, 'Can I please have a scoop of cookies and cream and a scoop of caramel, in a double chocolate cone?'

'I'll have the same,' Will says. He's still wearing the lipstick and pearls. Everyone around us is looking at him. But neither of us cares. Death does that, I think. It makes small things fall away.

At the end of the Corso, I take off my boots and socks, and skip down the steps, sinking my feet into the sand, wiggling my toes. I walk closer to the water and sit down, feeling the sand shift beneath me. Will sits beside me, his long legs outstretched.

As the sun sets behind us, the entire ocean seems to turn to glass.

'This has always been my favourite time of year to be in Sydney,' I say.

'Why? It's cold.'

'Because the water is still warm. Pa used to tell me it's because the sun lives under the sea at night, so even though the days get shorter, the water stays warm until the winter solstice, when the sun climbs out and the days start getting longer again.'

I look up at Will. He has ice cream smeared around his mouth.

'At least, I think that's how the story went.'

'It sounds like he was a great storyteller.'

Above, the first stars are appearing. They dot the sky like freckles on grey skin. 'Yeah, I forget that sometimes. He stopped telling stories after my nan died.'

Will slings his arm around me. It hangs awkwardly sweet.

sea daisy

I wake early on Thursday to an email from my supervisor telling me he's got no more feedback for me on my thesis. *Congratulations*, he writes.

I close the email, put my phone down and pick up my laptop off the desk. Opening it, I log into my university's student portal and navigate to my assessments page. There, I upload my thesis, watching a loading bar fill with blue. When it's ready, I click submit. Just like that, it's done.

I close the laptop, then return to bed.

And I wait. I wait for something to lift, for something to release. But this heaviness stays. Oppressive and cold, it's as if my bones are filled with lead. The pain of it is dark purple.

I roll over and face the wall. There's a watermark above my head. Like blotched skin. I close my eyes and eventually fall back asleep.

A few days later, I meet Adam at Central Station. We hug and he kisses me on the cheek. There's a distance between us that neither of us acknowledges. 'I thought we could go for a walk,' I say.

He shrugs. 'Sure.'

Up the road a little, we pass an Asian supermarket. The smell of dried sour plums, seaweed and five spice reminds me of being fifteen and walking through one of Hong Kong's wet markets with Charlotte, following Mavic and Elvie through the throng of people. We'd hold the shopping bags while they bartered for our groceries.

Mavic was Charlotte's second mum. She was five foot, with wide hips, a thick neck and arms that enveloped. And though she worked for their family the whole time I knew Charlotte, she never called the kids by their real names. For as long as Charlotte and I were best friends, Charlotte was 'Number One' and her brothers 'Number Two' and 'Number Three'.

Elvie, who worked for my family, had a sharp tongue and eyes that prodded you in the back. She wore oversized button-up shirts that hung on her like she was a wire coathanger. She meant business and, at first, I found her seriousness unnerving. But then, in the wake of my father shattering a glass coffee table, she took my hand in the kitchen and smiled in a way that made home bearable. Safer, somehow.

When I first arrived in Hong Kong, I couldn't stand the smells. The driver would take me past a wet market on the drive to school every morning and, even with the window closed, I'd hold my nose to block out the stink of raw meat and freshly gutted fish. But then I met Charlotte, and somehow that made the smells of Hong Kong seem exciting. Charlotte's parents loved that Mavic took us downtown to the market; I think they even suggested it. But when my mum found out Elvie was taking me with them, she told my dad and he fired her. In her place he hired Mae Grace, who would cook snake soup in our kitchen and eat it for lunch. Secretly, I loved that the thought of eating snake freaked out my dad.

I turn now to Adam. 'I'm just going to step in here for a sec, okay?'

Adam hesitates. 'Um, yeah,' he says. 'Sure.' And he follows me in.

I walk down the aisles, scanning the shelves. There are Hello Panda biscuits, cuttlefish crackers, dried squid and mochi. Adam hovers behind me nervously, as if he's not sure where to stand or what to look at.

'Yes, they have them!' I say, pouncing on some haw flakes. I buy a packet, and a handful of lychee cups.

'What are those?' Adam asks as I tear open the packet out on the street.

'Haw flakes,' I explain. 'They're made from Chinese hawthorn.'

'Chinese what?'

'Hawthorn. It's a fruit.'

I think of winter mornings, when the air was less dense, buying candied hawthorn from hawkers on street corners. Charlotte and I, lips scarlet and high on sugar, running circles around Mavic.

'Do you want to try one?' I ask Adam.

He gives me an incredulous look. 'No thanks,' he says.

I lean back against the shop's window.

'So, you said on the phone you wanted to talk,' Adam prompts. 'What about?'

Before I can reply he says, 'You're mad about the other night, aren't you?'

For a moment I don't know what he's talking about; I'd completely forgotten about our fight.

'I looked everywhere for you,' he says, sounding defensive.

'Wait, what?'

'You just got up from the table and left.'

'I was in the bathroom.'

'For twenty minutes?' he snaps.

And suddenly I realise he didn't know where I was at all. I imagine myself passed out, wrapped around the toilet bowl. A mess. Pathetic. My cheeks flush red. 'Sorry for leaving so abruptly,' I mumble.

'Yeah,' he says.

'But I didn't like what you said,' I continue. 'It was really unfair.'

He looks away from me, takes a deep breath. 'You're right. I'm sorry . . . I'm just stressed. Like, I don't know what I'm going to do now. I didn't get anything I applied for.'

I take hold of his hand, lace my fingers through his.

He says, 'And it's incredible, you know, that internship. I'd just hate to see you wasting it.' He squeezes my hand. 'I say it because I care.'

'I know.'

And then he adds, 'I love you, okay?' And I feel my body soften.

'Okay.'

'Are we all good then?'

'There's actually something else I wanted to tell you.'

'What's that?'

'My grandpa died.'

'What?' he says, startled. 'When?'

'Monday.'

'I'm so sorry to hear that,' he says. 'You should've called me.' He lets go of my hand and turns to face me, arms outstretched. 'Come here.' He pulls me towards him.

'Thanks,' I mutter into his shoulder.

Adam's fingers are in my hair, stroking the nape of my neck.

When he lets go, I tell him, 'The funeral is on Wednesday. My parents are landing tomorrow morning.'

'Do you want me to come?'

I shrug.

'Might be kind of weird, though. Like, I haven't met your parents before.'

We were on a break the last time my parents visited.

'Yeah,' I say. 'I guess.'

'I mean, I can,' he says quickly. 'If you want me to.'

I shake my head. 'Nah, don't worry about it,' I say, thinking the only thing worse than my father disliking Adam would be seeing them actually get along.

I peel open a lychee cup and slurp it up, sloshing the jelly around my mouth.

'Do you feel okay?' he asks at last.

'Yeah. Kind of numb, actually.'

'Mm, at least you and your grandfather weren't that close.'

'What?'

'I thought you didn't like living with him.'

I walk over to a bin and spit out the jelly. It's making me feel sick.

'He was still my grandpa, Adam.'

He sighs. 'Sorry, that came out wrong.'

I look away from him.

'I just don't really know what to say . . .'

He's never had someone close to him die, I realise, so I offer him a smile that says, *It's okay, I forgive you.*

'How about we go to mine?' he suggests. 'I'll run you a bath.'

'That'd be really nice,' I say. 'Thank you.'

Even though Adam lives with his parents, and even though we've been dating for four years, we still walk down the side path to get to his room. If we walk through the house, his mum will sit me down at the kitchen bench and insist on tea and biscuits. Occasionally she'll comment that I'm looking very thin, though never when Adam is within earshot.

I told Adam once, 'Your mum said she's worried I don't eat enough.'

He gave me a quizzical look, and then said, 'You're not *that* thin.'

And I knew he was right. I could be thinner.

We enter Adam's room and he flicks on the light. I say room, but really he has a floor, an entire floor, all to himself. It's all polished tiles and plush leather couches, with fine art on the walls and huge windows that overlook the harbour. He has a kitchenette. And an ensuite with the biggest bath I've ever seen. A projector instead of a TV.

I slide the glass door shut behind me and take off my shoes. My feet are cold on the tiles as I shuffle across to the couch. Sinking into it, I draw my knees up to my chin and wrap my arms around my legs, shivering a little. Adam kisses my forehead and goes to run the bath.

When it's ready, he picks me up off the couch and carries me into the bathroom. He's lit a candle, and now the bathroom smells of vanilla daisies. Adam lowers me to my feet, touches his hands to my hips, and slowly lifts up my jumper and shirt together. I raise my arms, letting him pull them over my head. He undoes the buttons on my jeans, and I pull them down, stepping out of them. As I stand before him in my bra and underwear, he gently presses his thumb against my hipbone. Rubbing it softly, back and forth.

I turn in his arms to face the mirror and catch my reflection. I look sick. Like a seashell that's had its flesh scooped out. I consider that aside from a few haw flakes this morning, I've barely eaten since Pa died. Every time I've tried, I've been overcome by nausea. Candlelight flickers against my cheeks, filling in the hollows with gold.

Adam turns his head so that we're both looking at ourselves. He grins and tells me we're a hot couple. And then he looks down at my body and whispers in my ear, 'You're so sexy.'

A wave of relief washes over me. I hold on to that. For better, or for worse.

I get out of the bath when my fingers begin to prune. Adam is watching a replay of a rugby league game in the other room, shouting at the TV intermittently, even though he knows who won. I dry off and put on underwear and the silk nightie he bought me for Valentine's Day. I keep it here because we so rarely sleep at my grandfather's apartment, Adam refusing to share a single bed with me. And also because the lace straps aren't actually that comfortable, so I wouldn't choose to wear it without him.

The bath drains in the ensuite and makes a loud gurgling sound. I hear Adam flick off the TV and walk down the hall into the bedroom. I turn on the lamp beside his bed and he turns off the ceiling light. Soft yellow surrounds us.

I put my wet hair up in a towel and recline on the bed. He undresses, leaving his clothes on the floor beside his washing basket.

Adam looks at me and smiles. Goosebumps prick my skin. He says, 'You look so perfect on my bed.'

I'm grinning. It's hurting my face.

He climbs onto the bed in his underwear and lies down beside me, stretching out an arm so that I can nestle into his side. I close my eyes, my cheek warm on his chest. I feel like I'm sinking. My bones are heavy and sore.

Adam brushes my cheek, traces the line of my jaw, my neck. He sweeps his fingertips across my breast, down the side of my ribcage, down to the hem of my nightdress. He slips a finger underneath, lifting the fabric over my hip so that it gathers around my waist. The sound of his breath deepening is pink turning into red. Bright red. Intense and full.

'Babe,' I say, my eyes still closed, 'I'm too tired.'

He smooths his hand across my backside. I feel him swelling against my thigh.

'I want you so bad,' he whispers.

I half smile. Because it feels good. This *wanting.* Being wanted like this.

And then he's kissing me, gently pulling down my underwear. Taking off his own. Spreading my legs.

He's on his knees now, his body looming over mine. A purple shadow stretches across the wall. He moves between my thighs, touches me, but I'm not that wet yet. In fact, I'm not wet at all. He pushes in and I gasp. It's like falling backwards in a dream. The way you wake suddenly. In a burst. Air rushing in.

'Does that feel good?' he asks, and I don't say anything, because it will feel good, eventually. If I let it. If I just relax.

And so I do. I surrender. And the good feelings start to creep in, intermingling with the bad, until I feel pleasure as much as pain. A blue equilibrium.

Afterwards, Adam curves his body around mine and tells me he loves me.

The moon outside is swollen, blood orange. The city sparkles underneath.

I excuse myself for the bathroom, shutting the door behind me, turning the tap on so he can't hear me pee.

When I wipe, there is a little blood on the toilet paper.

I don't have my period, though. This just happens sometimes.

sea lily

My parents arrive with a bouquet of lilies. They look immaculate: the flowers, my parents. They look immaculate, and I think that if it weren't for the flowers, you'd hardly guess there was any occasion for the visit.

Mum arranges them in a vase and sits the vase on the kitchen bench. It's a stunning bouquet, all pink and white, pink and white. Pink and ghost white.

She takes Dad's jacket, hangs it on a hook by the door.

Dad shivers, grunts. 'God, it's cold in here. Why isn't the heater on?'

I shrug.

'I thought I paid to get it fixed?' he says.

'It's not that cold,' I say.

'You just haven't acclimatised, honey,' Mum says to him. Then she turns to me. 'It's terribly hot in Singapore right now,' she explains, as if I never lived there, as if I was never dragged away from all my friends in Hong Kong, away from Charlotte. As if I've forgotten how hot and sticky my tears were.

Dad marches over to the heater and flicks it on full bore.

We go out for dinner in Manly, because neither of my parents cook and when I offer to, my dad asks, 'Why?' And then we go out for breakfast too, to a cafe on the beachfront, and since no one is talking about the funeral you'd almost be forgiven for thinking there isn't one.

When we get home, I go into my room and put on the outfit I wore with Will when we cleaned out Pa's room. I step into the living room in the suit, bright red socks and gold-embroidered boots. Mum looks me over, then says, 'I thought you could wear this.' From her suitcase she pulls a shiny bag, and from that she pulls pink tissue paper, and from that she pulls a floral-print dress. White lilies floating in a sea of teal silk.

'But I like what I'm wearing,' I say.

'I think it would be nicer if you wore a dress,' she says.

'I'm comfortable in this.'

'Olivia,' Mum says, holding the dress out, 'I bought it for *you*.'

'I already have an outfit.'

My dad walks out of Pa's room in a sharp black suit. He eyes my outfit. Scowls. 'Put the dress on, Olivia,' he says over the top of my mother's next sentence.

'But—' I begin.

'Your "outfit" is inappropriate,' he says. 'End of conversation.'

'Fine,' I say, defeated, and take the dress from my mum.

As always when I put on a dress my mother has bought me, it's a size too small. I have to suck in my stomach to do up the zip.

Only a few friends ever visited Pa while I'd been living with him, and my parents haven't invited any of them to the funeral. At the cemetery in Fairlight, just ten minutes from the apartment in Manly where Pa lived his entire life, it's just us, the neighbours Will and Annie, and two of my dad's business associates. I wonder if Pa cares, but then realise he's dead, so how could he?

We gather around a hole in the ground and watch as a sleek black coffin is lowered into it. He's being buried beside Nan, and though I'm sure he can't feel anything, and that it doesn't really matter how close or how far his plot is from hers, I can't help but mourn the metre and a half of earth between them. Because even when his coffin breaks down around him, as it inevitably will, and the soil fills the holes in his sunken flesh, there'll forever be a metre and a half of dirt and worms and bugs and rocks between his bones and her bones. And there's something awfully painful about that thought. It makes me feel like I'm full of earth myself. Feeling it everywhere. In my ears, my nose, under my tongue. Grit between my teeth. Black sand under my fingernails.

The first shovel of soil lands on a wreath of white lilies and my mum bursts into tears. It's perfectly timed. And then another shovel of soil, and her cries thicken, become heavier, wetter somehow. Dad puts his arm around her shoulders. The colour of her wail is an uncomfortable red. Red like wet autumn leaves, muddy and rotting.

'Come on, now,' Dad says, patting her on the shoulder. 'Come on . . . enough now.'

Dad has booked dinner at a fancy restaurant in the city and invited his two business associates. It's one of those places with a degustation menu, one of those places where someone is paid to match every course with a different bottle of wine. One of those places where you don't ask to change an ingredient, because that would throw out the whole dish. That would offend the chef.

'I can't eat that,' I say, as a plate of beef cheeks is placed on the table in front of me. 'I'm a vegetarian.'

My dad very nearly spits his wine back into his glass. 'You're a what?'

'A vegetarian. I don't eat meat.'

'Since when?' he says, his eyes darting from his business associates, to me, to the beef cheeks, back to the associates. His eyes apologising to them. His eyes punishing me.

'A year ago,' I lie. I ate a chicken salad yesterday. In fact, I ate smoked salmon this morning. But there's something about the colour of the beef cheeks that makes me think of Pa's muddy flesh.

Outside, the clouds are backlit with fierce gold. The same gold that adorns my mum's neck. The same gold that makes her earlobes sag. The weight of it. Her watch. Her rings. Her bangles. Gold. Gold. Gold.

'We'll ask for something else,' Mum says.

'Absolutely not,' Dad says.

'Simon, I think—' she begins.

He cuts her off. 'Don't.' My father glares at me. 'Olivia, do you know how hard it was to get a table here?'

'No,' I mutter.

'What?'

'I said no!'

Hot red flushes down his neck. '*You* are embarrassing yourself.'

And I want to say, *I'm not embarrassed.*

But then I look at his hand, resting on the table; I look at how he's gripping the fork, his knuckles white. I know that hand. I know how it stings. How it burns across the cheek. And so I don't say, *I'm not embarrassed.* I don't say anything at all. I just pick up my knife and my fork, and I slice the cheek in half.

I chew the flesh, the muddy flesh, chew and swallow.

'Olivia has an internship at Lazard,' Mum says brightly, changing the subject. She's good at that, good at diffusing.

Dad relaxes his grip on the fork.

'That's great news,' says one of the associates, and the muscles around Dad's eyes begin to slacken.

Mum continues, 'She just finished her degree in economics.'

'You're finishing in May?' says the other associate, addressing the question to me.

'I took one subject part-time in first year,' I explain. 'That's why I'm finishing half way through the year.'

'She handed in her thesis early,' Mum adds.

The associate looks at my dad, smiles. 'Impressive.'

'Yes,' my mum says, 'we're very proud. Aren't we, Simon?'

I sit back in my chair, look out the window at fading gold.

'Yes,' Dad says.

Gold turning into grey.

It's the same offhand *yes* he gave to the waiter asking, *Do you want cracked pepper on your soup?*

Then my dad turns to one of his associates and asks him about his work in coal. The associate's forehead is studded with sweat. He has a thick neck that wobbles beneath the chin when he speaks. He tells my dad the coal industry is thriving in spite of this greenie nonsense. Swathes of people across the globe are still living without access to electricity, he says, quoting statistics. The numbers surprise me. He says access to electricity should be a human right, and coal is cheap. For that reason, for now, it's our best option. All he's really doing is ensuring *everyone* can afford electricity.

And for a moment, it almost sounds heroic.

My parents leave Sydney before the lilies in the living room have even begun to wilt. Alone in the apartment again, I make myself a cup of tea and take it out onto the balcony, which overlooks the wharf and the old aquarium. A ferry is pulling in. Behind it, a fleet of yachts are racing towards the heads. I think of the *Sea Rose.*

'*Shit,*' I whisper, realising I never called Mac to tell him I couldn't come with him to fetch his boat and sail her home. I wonder if his friend was offended.

I go into my room and grab my phone. His name is saved in my contacts as *Mac the kidnapper.*

He picks up on the second ring. 'Mac, here,' he says, his voice deep blue.

'Hey, it's Olivia.'

'Oli!' he shouts. 'How are ya, kid?'

'I'm okay. How are you?'

'Great!'

I laugh; his enthusiasm is infectious. 'That's good. Sorry I didn't call last week . . .'

'No worries. Maggie reckoned I overdid it with the whole sailing to New Zealand thing.'

'The kidnapping.'

He cracks up. 'Yeah, yeah. Something like that.'

There's a moment's silence, then he says, 'Well, I'm just happy to hear from ya,' and I feel the knots loosen.

'How was your sail back to the CYC?'

'It turns out old *Sea Rose* took longer to clean than expected. We're not bringing her back till tomorrow.'

'Oh,' I say, 'does that mean I can still come then? Please?'

'We'll pick you up at eight.'

sea violet

The wind is cutting sideways when I step outside the following morning. As I walk with Mac out to the street he tells me we're going to have a wild ride. I feel my chest expanding. A pulling that is as exciting as it is terrifying.

When I get to the car, there is a woman in the front seat. She has long silver hair pulled back into a braid.

'This is Maggie,' Mac says as I climb into the back. The woman turns around. She's wearing thick black sunglasses. Gazing vaguely in my direction, Maggie extends her hand. I reach across. And in the moment my skin touches hers, there's an unfolding, and a closing-up. Like the sky is spreading out, getting bigger. Like the earth is contracting, getting smaller. Our bodies drawing nearer, closer, until it's just her and I. Her and I.

'I'm Maggie,' she says. Her voice is a colour I've never seen before. *Maggie*. Velvet lilac.

She is wild violets in the tundra.

'I'm Oli.'

She smiles. 'I know.'

Half an hour's drive north of Pa's apartment, we pull up at the Royal Prince Alfred Yacht Club, nestled on the banks of Pittwater. Lines of yachts pattern the sky with their masts, stripes of stiff white. I feel giddy with excitement.

When Mac pulls up the handbrake, a dog sticks its head up between Maggie's knees. The sudden sight of it scares the shit out of me. I squeal.

Maggie is still facing forwards, gazing out the window, as she has been the entire drive. She laughs, patting the dog's head. 'This is Coco,' Maggie says.

Coco is all sleek black fur with big button eyes. Chubby, even for a labrador.

'Hey, there,' I say.

Coco wags her tail eagerly. It thumps against the dashboard.

'She's very excited,' says Maggie, still facing forwards. 'We rarely make new friends.'

Mac gets out of the car and opens my door. I climb out and follow him around to the back of the car where we unload two bags from the boot. From where I'm standing, I see Maggie open her door. Coco leaps out onto the concrete. Maggie follows, carrying some sort of harness. She calls Coco to her feet, then she reaches down and fits the harness to the dog. And it hits me.

Maggie is blind. Like, *really* blind.

And yet she strides off confidently with Coco, calling back to us, 'Well? Are you coming?'

I look down at my feet rooted to the pavement. I'm rendered speechless.

'Told you,' Mac whispers, a smile spreading. 'She's *incredible*.'

I nod wordlessly and he laughs, pats me on the back. 'Let's go, kid.'

We follow Maggie and Coco down the dock to where the *Sea Rose* is tied up in her berth. How Coco found this boat among all the other boats is beyond me.

Maggie undoes Coco's harness, chucks it on deck, then climbs up and over the lifelines. Coco jumps up and follows Maggie into the cockpit. Sitting down, Coco licks Maggie's ankles. Maggie grins and pats the dog on the head. 'Love you too, hon.'

Mac and I climb on board. 'Up here,' he says, motioning for me to follow him up to the front of the yacht. 'Shoes off first, though,' he says.

I untie my sneakers, pull them off and leave them in the cockpit, then join Mac up front.

'Have you sailed before? Other than last week, I mean?'

'My family used to holiday on a yacht,' I tell him.

'What kind of yacht?'

I shrug.

'Did it have sails?'

'No, only a motor.'

'That doesn't count then.'

'Because it didn't have sails?'

'Thank you, Captain Obvious,' he says. 'Motor yachts make noise. They churn water, spit exhaust. Sailing—and I mean *real* sailing—is about listening.'

'Sure.'

'The first step in learning to sail is finding out how much you don't know.'

'Well, I don't know anything,' I say.

Maggie laughs, calls out from the cockpit, 'Great answer!'

I feel something swelling in me. I giggle.

'The second step is learning that the ocean and wind are unknowable.'

'What does that mean?'

'It means that no matter what you think you know, you must always be open to the unexpected. I've been sailing my entire life, and yet the older I get, the more the sea surprises me.'

Maggie yells, 'Go easy on her, Mac!'

'I think that makes sense,' I say.

'The third and final thing is this: you can't change the wind. Okay? All you can do is learn to adjust the sails.'

'But you can look at forecasts, no?'

'What was lesson number two?'

'Expect the unexpected?'

'Exactly. Boats sink when people think they can control the wind, control the sea. But sailing isn't about control. It's about listening, *feeling*, surrendering, and adapting.'

Maggie chimes in. 'It's also about getting wet and cold while going nowhere fast.'

Mac knows the *Sea Rose* like it's an extension of himself—the way I imagine you'd know a lover after fifty years of nights. How you'd learn to see them in the dark.

I help him raise the big sail, which he calls the main, by pulling on a thick red rope. When the sail reaches the top of the mast, he seems to open out with it, his chest broadening, his smile widening.

'See that?' he says, pointing across the bow to a dark patch of rippled sea. 'That's wind.'

I watch the dark patch fan out across the bay. It moves closer; closer still. Mac counts down, 'Four, three, two,' and as he whispers, 'one,' the dark touches the edge of the boat. The gust rises, fills the sail. The *Sea Rose* strains, then lifts at the edge, pulls forwards.

'Beautiful,' he says, eyeing the sail, all white and spread out flat against the ruffled grey sky.

I follow Mac back down into the cockpit where Maggie is sitting at the wheel, steering, Coco at her ankles. Fitted to the cockpit near where she's seated, an audio compass is voicing information aloud for her.

Sailing is about listening.

A flock of seagulls passes over us, their shadows hitting Maggie's face. Can you feel a shadow?

'If you could be an animal, what animal would you be?' she asks.

'I don't know,' I answer honestly.

Maggie says, 'I'd be a whale,' and Mac cracks up.

'You can't sing,' he says.

'I could if I was a whale.'

'What would Coco be?'

'She's a dog, Mac. She'd be a dog.'

I laugh, then ask her, 'What kind of whale?'

'A humpback.'

'Why?'

'They swim from the Coral Sea all the way down to Antarctica every year. What a journey!'

'I'd be an albatross,' Mac declares. 'The same as Robynne.'

I ask Maggie, 'Did you know Robynne?'

'Know her? I knew her first!'

'So you two met through Robynne?'

Mac chuckles. 'You could say that.'

'Robynne and I took a gap year before gap years were a thing,' Maggie explains. 'At least, certainly before they were a thing for women. And so we turned up on the beach at Bondi, two wide-eyed Brits, and found that there weren't any girls swimming—they were only sunbathing. Robynne didn't care, of course. She just marched into the waves. I followed. We got sand everywhere. Almost drowned. Then this guy and his sister had to come in for us.' She points to Mac. 'Couldn't stop laughing.'

Mac smiles. 'Couldn't believe my luck.'

'Robynne sounds like a lot of fun,' I say.

'Oh, she was,' says Maggie. 'She was a riot.'

'What happened to her?'

Silence pools in the cockpit.

'I'm sorry,' I say, regretting the question.

'Don't be,' Mac says, patting me on the back.

'My grandpa died last week,' I blurt out.

A gust ripples through the quiet on deck. It catches in the sail, like a butterfly in a net. Pulling on a rope at her feet, Maggie draws the boom pole in. Everything tightens. We pick up speed.

'Oh, Oli,' she says, 'I'm so sorry to hear that.'

We're nearing the heads of Pittwater now, swells are climbing up out of the deep. The *Sea Rose* rises and falls. Rises and falls.

'I found him.'

Maggie taps the seat, motioning for me to sit with her. I shuffle across the cockpit, squeeze in beside her. She puts her arm around my shoulder, draws me in, so tenderly. Like I'm becoming a part of her, a part of her body, a fold of skin. It's warm and round and full. Mac comes and sits on my other side. With both arms, he envelops Maggie and me. Three become one. Rising and falling.

And the weight, this crushing weight I've been carrying, is lifted. Because they hold me in a way that lets me let go of myself. In them, I come undone. I burst into tears. The sound that comes out of me is creamy blue.

'Someone told me a special story about death,' Maggie says. 'She told me that we are like rivers, all of us. We begin as clouds, and then one day, we rain down and become a trickle. We grow into a stream . . . thicken into a river. We travel great distances, wind through all kinds of valleys and forests. Sometimes we come together with other rivers, flow together, swirl together in great lakes, part ways, flow alone . . . But we all meet again in the end at the river mouth, where we empty into the sea.'

I think of all the years Pa's river flowed with Nan's, how heartbreaking it must have been when their rivers parted ways. Creamy blue cries wet my cheeks, wet Mac's sleeve, but it feels good, to empty like this. I imagine Nan and Pa meeting at the river mouth, swirling together, blue and gold.

'Who told you that story?' I ask.

Mac answers, 'Robynne.'

Maggie nods.

'Robynne disappeared one night in the Southern Ocean,' Mac says.

I feel my insides lurch. 'Disappeared?' Wondering how a body made up of memories and desires could just dissolve. Like ice into the grey.

Mac takes a deep breath. 'It was just the two of us on board. We were thirty years old and sailing the world.' He pauses. Closes his eyes with the memory. 'I woke up for watch and she was gone.'

'Gone?' I whisper. 'I don't understand.'

Mac holds us tighter. 'I know it sounds strange, but I hope it wasn't an accident. I like to think it was her decision.'

'Really?'

'Yeah,' he tells me. 'I mean, I know she loved me. She absolutely did. And I loved her. She knew that. But she had dark days . . . I like to believe she made a choice.'

I breathe in. We choose to breathe, don't we?

I imagine Mac waking up for watch. The panic. Searching a monochrome for detail. The ocean like a painting. A site for yearning.

I shudder. 'Don't you wish you could go back? To try to stop her? Save her, even?'

'I did wish that. For many years. But the worst feeling in the world is wanting to go back to another time. Because it takes you out of time—out of *this* time.' Mac wipes his eyes. 'Me and Robynne . . . our time will come again. At the river mouth.'

Maggie takes my hand. I am shaking, I realise. She holds me until I am still.

'Life is a series of happy and unhappy endings, Oli. But it is also a series of beginnings . . . Never forget that.'

sea tulip

After we dock the *Sea Rose* at the CYC, we cross the road and walk up the hill a little way to Mac and Maggie's apartment. The sky is a tangle of grey clouds, hot pink at the edges. 'What a beautiful evening,' Maggie says in the dying light.

I look at her. 'I don't mean to be rude, but . . .'

'But how do I know the sky looks beautiful right now?'

'Is that a stupid question?'

'I have synaesthesia,' Maggie says. 'It's where you see colours when you think of or hear sounds, words, numbers—even time.'

Mac chimes in. 'Cool, huh?'

'My sight degenerated when I was in my forties, and I was blind by fifty. But I still see colours that don't exist in the real world. I see space in colour, voices in colour.'

I think of my cries, creamy blue. The number one, pale yellow. Wednesdays, blood orange. Maggie, velvet lilac.

'I see colours with all those things, too,' I say, and Maggie holds out her hand in the direction of my voice. I clasp it in mine.

Softly, she says, 'I knew we'd made a special friend.'

Maggie and Mac's apartment is like an art gallery. They have everything from Australian landscapes painted by First Nations Peoples, to prints of Matisse's dancers, modern minimalist works, and contemporary photographs of blackened glaciers. Sandstone sculptures of breasts and arched hips. Maggie explains that her parents were artists and that she'd been a curator in London.

'A very good one,' Mac adds.

She tells me how when Robynne disappeared, she flew to New Zealand to get Mac and bring him back to London with her.

'She saved my life,' Mac says.

'And then he saved mine,' says Maggie, describing the deep depression she'd fallen into when she started to lose her sight. Mac, by then living back in Australia and building the *Sea Rose*, had gone to London for Maggie, eventually bringing her out here to live with him. In their own way, they guided each other through grief, through the dark, back into colour.

Mac makes pasta while Maggie and I drink tea in the living room. Wafts of hot garlic fill the room. On the shelf behind Maggie are more books than I've ever seen in a home. Cascading over them are vines that hang from the ceiling. It's a library of words and flowers. And all along the windowsills are glass jars with succulents, their roots like tentacles in water flowerbeds.

Maggie says, 'Mac tells me you're an artist.'

I laugh. 'Kind of. I mean, I liked painting in school. And drawing. I wanted to study art, but I haven't painted myself in ages.'

'Do you know what makes an artist?' she asks. 'Or a work of art?'

I shrug, then realise she can't see me shrug. 'Not really.'

'An artist is a person who can see the world from a different angle,' she says. 'So I think a piece of art is an object as complex and as multifaceted as reality.' She takes off her sunglasses. Her eyes are milky sky. 'Oli, tell me: which is your favourite?'

I look around the room, my eyes settling on a framed Yves Klein print. 'The blue monochrome,' I say.

'Why?'

'Because it's . . . I don't know. Because it's everything and nothing.'

She laughs. 'It's my favourite too.'

'Why?'

'Like you said, it's everything and nothing. Because no matter how brilliant and bold and *present* the blue is, it is always about absence, always about something unknown, something *beyond* you.'

'Exactly!' I say.

Mac calls out from the kitchen, 'Glad that made sense to you, Oli, because I've got no idea what she's talking about.'

Maggie chuckles, shakes her head.

'You know, I think being blind is a little like the monochrome. The absence of detail. People fear it. They fear going blind. But when you've lived with blindness for as long as I have, you realise there is still *seeing*, it's just seeing differently. In that way, being blind is an art.'

'You see the world from a different angle.'

Mac sticks his head out of the kitchen, and says, 'All I see when I look at it is the ocean.'

'I've never seen the ocean *that* blue before,' I say.

Maggie smiles. 'You haven't been to the Coral Sea then.'

I shake my head. 'Where's that?'

'Queensland,' she says. 'Mac takes *Sea Rose* up every winter. We do Hamilton Island and Magnetic Island race weeks. Though we're not really racing; we always come last.'

Mac interrupts to insist, 'This year will be different!'

'He says that every year. Really, we just go because we're old and, well, why the hell not?'

I stare into the monochrome and imagine diving into that blue. Being in it. 'I'd love to go one day.'

'Why don't you come with us?' says Maggie.

I open my mouth to speak. Hesitate.

'When are you leaving?' I ask.

'At the end of next week.'

'How long does it take to get there?'

'It's possible to do it in a week, but at the pace we go it tends to be more like three.'

'I start my internship in two weeks.'

Maggie frowns. 'I thought you weren't going to do it?'

Mac comes into the living room with two plates of pasta, hands one to each of us. 'I said she was *considering* not doing it.'

'Well,' Maggie says, 'the offer stands.'

'I'll think about it,' I tell her.

'I hope you do. The Coral Sea is magic in winter.'

sea poppy

I turn up at Adam's house on Friday afternoon in loose trousers and a baggy jumper. I've got my period and my breasts are sore, so I'm wearing a sports bra for comfort.

The sun is setting over the harbour. The water is rippled orange. Adam is on his balcony with an open beer can on the table. When he sees me walk through the side gate onto the balcony, he says, 'The boys are all going to the pub.'

'I thought we were just going to chill and watch a movie.'

'Well, that was before I knew they were going to the pub.'

'I'm really tired,' I say.

'Liv, *all* my friends are going.'

And I want to say, *My grandpa just died. It's been a hell of a week. I'm fucking exhausted.* But I don't, because he's getting up from his chair, walking over to me. And kissing me. Kissing me. Kissing me. Kissing me. And then he's asking, 'Are you gonna wear that?'

I walk into the pub behind Adam. It smells of beer-sodden coasters and worn carpet. He orders me a glass of wine, even though I tell him I don't feel like drinking, then we carry our drinks over to a table where five guys in suits are sitting. Jake, a new friend of the group whom I've met at least three times, introduces himself to me.

'Nice to meet you,' he says.

'Yup,' I say, as Adam pulls out a seat for me. I sit down beside him, take a sip of wine.

Henry, the only one in the group who doesn't drink, says, 'Hey, Olivia. How are you?'

And when I say, 'Pretty tired, actually,' the conversation falls dead, so I perk up. 'But other than that, I'm good! How are you?'

'Yeah, great. Just started at Deutsche Bank. Tiring, but a lot of fun. Adam said you've got an internship at Lazard? That's unreal.'

'Yeah, thanks. I start next week.'

'Exciting.' He raises his soda. 'Cheers.' We clink glasses. I pretend to take a sip. And then Henry turns to Jake and they start talking about the shares Jake has just invested in. A big risk. Willing to lose. The pay-off would be huge.

After a while, my back starts to hurt. These stools are awfully uncomfortable.

'Don't you like the wine?' Adam says, slurring a little. The whisky on his breath is enough to make your eyes sting.

I shrug. And then I see Jake pass Adam something under the table.

And it's not like this is new—but I'm tired. That whole body tired you get after spending too much time in the sun. And I just don't want to deal with a coked-up Adam telling me the same story again and again and again.

I'm sweaty, now. God, I'm sweaty. I'm burning up. Wearing this stupid jumper that I can't take off because all I've got on underneath is a fucking sports bra.

I get out my phone and text him. *I swear to god, if that's what I think it is, I'm leaving.*

His phone pings in his pocket. He whips it out. 'Oh look, I've got a text from Olivia. That's funny considering she's sitting right beside me.'

Jake laughs. 'Read it out!'

I hunch over, duck my head. Surely he won't.

He absolutely will.

'*I swear to god, if that's what I think it is, I'm leaving*,' Adam reads.

I raise my eyes, look at him.

He meets my gaze. 'Alright—piss off then.'

It's raining when I get out of the cab. Tears and sky mixing together on my cheeks. I get inside and find a notice taped to the door of the lift. *Out of service. Management apologises for the inconvenience.*

By the time I reach my apartment on the seventh floor, my thighs are burning. I unlock the door, walk in and lie down on the living room floor. Rolling onto my back, I wipe my eyes and then blow my nose on my jacket sleeve. Staring at the ceiling, I notice watermarks, like blooms of algae. I remember Maggie's words. *The Coral Sea is magic in winter.* I think of the ceiling becoming water. Raining down. Becoming a night sky, flecked with stars. How wide and open it must all feel. Up there, in a sea of coral flowers. How *magic.*

I get out my phone.

Mac picks up on the second ring.

'It's Oli,' I say. 'I've changed my mind. Can I still come with you to the Coral Sea?'

'Wouldn't have it any other way.'

sea dandelion

I'm on the balcony nursing a cup of green tea when I hear a knock at my front door. I take a sip, but the tea is still burning hot. I wince. Swallow. It scalds my throat. My chest hurts.

There's another knock. 'Liv!' I hear him call through the door.

I get up; my legs are shaky. I walk through the apartment with soft, careful steps, unsure yet if I'm going to open the door. There've been two days of silence, but it's Sunday afternoon now, and the party's over; his friends have all gone home and he's starting to miss me. This understanding is at once familiar and shocking. It's like looking down and seeing a wound: that moment in which the mind wakes up to the body, and you suddenly feel the pain.

I put my tea down on the table but, distracted, I sit it too close to the edge and it falls off. The ceramic mug cracks on the floor.

'Liv!' he yells. 'I know you're in there!'

I grab a tea towel to mop up the spilt tea.

'Please!' he begs. 'Just open the door.'

I put the pieces of broken cup in the bin and walk to the door. Looking through the peephole, I see his eyelids are puffy, his face flushed pink. There are marks beneath his eyes, making the blue of them stand out like a lit flare.

I open the door and ease myself out, closing the door behind me, so that we're on the landing.

He pulls me into a hug. And then he kisses me. It's sour. My nose is blocked from all the crying, but I can still smell cigarette smoke on his clothes. I push his face away. 'Get off me.'

'Liv . . .' he whispers, shrinking back, hurt. He takes hold of my hand, squeezes it gently. He sighs. His breath stinks. I need air.

'Come on,' I say, 'let's go for a walk.'

I begin to descend the stairs, but he doesn't follow. I pause on the lower landing and turn to look up at him, a flight of stairs above me now.

'Can't we stay here?'

'No,' I say adamantly, in a voice I hardly recognise.

'You don't even have shoes on.'

'I don't care,' I retort and continue down the stairs.

He hurries after me, catching up to me in the foyer, where I charge through the front door of the building without waiting for him.

On the street, I march down the hill into the heart of town, Adam half a step behind. We walk in silence all the way to the beach, where I sink my feet into the cold sand and sit down, wrapping my arms around my torso. Holding myself together.

Adam sits down beside me. 'I honestly didn't think you'd be this upset.'

'I'm not upset,' I snap.

'Okay, well, what was that all about then?' He touches a hand to my shoulder and I edge away. This time his shock transforms into anger. 'You know, you're just as much in the wrong as I am,' he says.

'*What?*'

'You embarrassed me in front of my friends.'

And I want to say, *Adam, you* humiliated *me,* but I can't bring myself to speak. I open my mouth, but nothing comes out.

Being humiliated does that to people: it silences them.

'I just don't know why you had a problem with a tiny bit of coke.'

'I wasn't in the mood.'

'What, so I can't have fun because you're in a *mood*?'

I hate how he says it: *mood*—like it's something non-human.

'I just think you could have shown a little more empathy.'

'You want me to have more *feelings*?'

As he says that I blink and my tears run free.

'Should I start crying now, too?'

'Fuck you.'

That makes him laugh. 'Come on . . .' He slips an arm around my waist, drawing me in close. 'This is us, Liv! We fight. And then we make up. And then we fight. And then we make up.'

'Well, maybe I don't like *us*,' I say.

He loosens his grip. I can feel him staring at me. I shiver.

'What's that supposed to mean?'

I shrug. I'm sobbing now.

'Look, if you don't want to be with me,' he says, in a very faraway voice, 'just say.'

I mumble, 'I don't want to be with you.' It's barely audible.

'What?'

'I said, I don't want to be with you anymore.'

At that moment, a crowd starts to cheer further down the beach. I look up to see a man down on one knee by the shoreline, a woman standing ankle deep in the water, laughing.

Adam has seen it too. He looks back to me and says, 'Well, that's fucking ironic, isn't it?'

I don't say anything. I just put my face in my hands, closing my eyes. The sand shifts beside me. When I finally look up, Adam is gone.

Back at the apartment, I punch in the code to let myself into the building, then ascend the stairs. When I get to the front door, I realise I'd gone out without my keys. I knock on Annie's door and Will opens it. He takes one look at me and says, 'Shit. Are you okay?'

'I need the spare key.'

He fetches it for me then says, 'Are you sure you're okay?'

I say, 'I think I just broke up with Adam.'

'Oh. Like, proper?'

I nod.

'Want me to come over?'

'No,' I say. 'I'm alright. I just need to be alone.'

He gives me a hug and tells me, 'Well, I'm here if you need anything.'

'Thanks,' I say, and let myself in.

When I close the door behind me, everything becomes deathly silent. I feel naked. Like a dandelion flower when all its seeds have been blown away. And so I pile on layers of clothes and blankets, building a protective shell around myself. But it's no use. I feel impossibly exposed.

Eventually, I fall asleep.

sea orchid

The night before we set sail, I stay at Maggie and Mac's and help them prepare the food for our voyage. We pre-cook meals to eat over the first week. 'After that,' Mac says, 'we get crafty with non-perishables.'

By midnight, the kitchen bench is stacked with Tupperware containers: vegetarian casseroles, an eggplant curry, spicy pumpkin soup.

Mac puts the last container in the fridge, then asks me if I've told my parents that I'm leaving.

'I sent them an email this morning telling them I turned down the internship.'

'What do you reckon they'll say?'

'Who knows?' I say. 'My dad already pretends I don't exist.'

Maggie, standing beside me in the kitchen, hugs me, holding my body against hers. 'Nope,' she says. 'I can feel you. You definitely exist.'

When I wake on the couch, sunlight is yellow yolk, flooding the room. Maggie emerges from her bedroom with Coco. The light catches Maggie's hair. It glints rose gold.

In her nightdress, she drifts through the yellow like she's underwater.

She stops in front of the bookshelf. Coco sits at her feet, waiting. 'Oli,' says Maggie, 'we need to choose which books to take with us.'

'Sure thing,' I say, getting up off the couch. Mac appears from his room, rubbing sleep from his eyes, as I scan the bookshelf. There are books on history and philosophy, adventure novels, and as many art catalogues as you'd find in a gallery bookshop. 'It's an impressive collection,' I say.

'Thank you. There wasn't a single book in this house before I got here.' Maggie laughs. 'I swear he'd never read a book in his life.'

'I'm a simple man.'

'Now he reads to me.'

'She opened my eyes,' Mac says, warm as the morning sun.

'Can you please find *The Lost Lunar Baedeker* by Mina Loy, and *Selected Poems* by H.D.?' Maggie asks. 'Poetry books are on the top shelf.'

I point them out and Mac pulls them down.

'Also, *A Field Guide to Getting Lost* by Rebecca Solnit.'

I find it on the shelf. The book is so worn the blue mountains on the cover are as thin and watery as sky. I open it. There are coffee stains on the title page.

Maggie says, 'My favourite book of all time. I think you'll feel the same. There's an excellent essay about Yves Klein. I'd love for you to read it to me.'

I put the book with the poetry collections, then Maggie invites me to choose a few for myself. I find Tim Winton's *Island Home* and Virginia Woolf's *The Waves.* I tell Maggie my choices, admitting I haven't read either. 'They have beautiful covers,' I say.

'Describe them to me,' she says, and so I do.

'*Island Home* has a photo of a beach. Bird's-eye view. Sand becoming ocean. And there's a tiny person walking with a tiny dog. It could be you and Coco!' I say. '*The Waves* has a photo of the sea—taken from the beach, I think, looking out. It's all silver and blue. You can't see the sun itself, but here and there you can see its light reflected on the waves.'

'Beautiful,' says Maggie. 'Mac, what are you bringing?'

'One of my favourites,' he says, pulling a novel from the shelf.

'I bet it's *Lost and Found*,' she whispers to me.

'*Lost and Found*, by Brooke Davis,' he says. 'It's about a young girl who goes on an adventure with a couple of old farts. They're mad!'

Maggie laughs. 'Sounds just like us!'

We pass through the heads, tack the *Sea Rose*, angle north. The sea is corrugated iron. Maggie is at the helm, steering us up the coast. *Sailing is about listening.*

Mac comes on deck with two bottles of nail polish. He calls me over. 'Port,' he says, holding up the red bottle. 'And starboard.' He waves the green bottle. 'It'll help you remember.'

'Why don't you just say left and right, and then I won't need to *remember*,' I say.

'Because you're a sailor now, so you gotta start talking like one.'

Maggie chimes in, 'Life at sea has its own language.'

'She's right,' Mac says. 'Walk into any yacht club in the world, and it won't matter who you are or what you look like—if you speak the language, you'll never feel out of place.'

'Fine,' I say, taking a seat in the cockpit.

Mac passes me the bottles. 'Red is your left foot. Green is your right foot.'

I start painting my toenails, a task I find tricky enough on dry land. Out here, with the boat chopping through swells, rocking back and forth, I paint as much of my toes as I do my toenails. 'Couldn't you have got me to do this before we left?'

Mac laughs. 'Where's the fun in that?'

For our first lunch at sea, we boil rice to eat with our eggplant curry. Sitting together in the cockpit, we eat from bowls in our laps. Mac takes over at the helm so Maggie can use both hands to eat. 'I'm bloody good for a blind sailor,' she says, 'but no one's *that* good.'

I've almost finished my curry when something comes undone at the bow of the boat. The headsail comes loose and begins flapping wildly like a bird in frenzy. Mac jumps up and hurries to the front of the boat. He calls out to me, 'Oli, give us a hand, would ya?'

I help him wind in the headsail. We pull in a rope that's now dragging along in the water. He inspects the end of the line. 'Ah, shit,' he says, 'think we lost a carabiner.'

'Sorry,' I say, knowing it was my knot that came undone.

'Don't worry, I should have double-checked it.'

Maggie calls out, 'If you don't know knots, tie lots.'

'No,' Mac says. 'If you don't know knots, you sit in the cockpit and practise until you do.' He ties off the headsail, takes me into the cockpit and gives me a coil of rope. First he demonstrates how to do a half-hitch. 'One hundred of those, please.' And then he shows me a figure-of-eight knot. 'One hundred of those, too.'

'What is this? Boot camp?'

'This is serious stuff, kid. When things go wrong at sea, they get very bad very quickly. You gotta learn to tie the ropes the right way.'

And so I do. For the next two hours, I sit on my arse, tying and untying knots until my hands are chafed.

'Show me your half-hitch,' Mac says.

I show him.

'Good. And your figure of eight?'

I show him that too.

He grins. 'Good work, kid.'

And though my skin is stinging raw, I feel my fingertips tingling with pride.

Mac takes the rope from me and puts it back in the bag it came from beneath his seat in the cockpit.

'Now what?' I say, and they both crack up. 'What's so funny?'

'At sea,' Maggie says, 'hours pass differently.'

'There's a whole lot of nothing,' Mac adds.

'So what do we do?'

Maggie smiles. 'You learn to be inventive with time.'

Maggie moves back to the steering wheel as Mac takes our plates below deck. He returns with the logbook.

We come up with a game in which we score points for various achievements made on board. Mac writes the rules in the back of the notebook. We begin with animals: thirty points if you see a shark; fifteen points for whales. Forty points for the fastest speed of the day. And then there are points for ticking over specific distances while you're at the helm. One hundred miles, ten points. Five hundred miles, fifty points. One thousand miles, one hundred points.

'How will I get any points if I'm never steering?' I ask. 'That means I can only get points for spotting animals.'

'You'll be at the helm soon enough,' Mac promises. Beyond him, the sun is setting, spilling open on distant mountains, coating them in liquid light. 'But for now, we're anchoring.'

Mac takes over at the helm and steers us into the harbour in Newcastle, where we find a mooring. 'When you're ready, we'll be able to sail through the night. You and I will take turns on watch. Four hours on, four hours off.'

'When will I be ready?'

'When I can fall asleep.'

'What do you mean?'

'Oli, when someone is on watch, you're putting your life in their hands. You need to trust them fully if you want to fall asleep.'

After we anchor, I see Maggie, standing at the stern, blow a kiss into the air.

'Who was that for?'

'Coco,' she says, smiling sweetly, 'I'm just wishing her goodnight.'

I blow a kiss into the air to Coco, who I imagine is right now settling down to sleep at the holiday kennel we dropped her off at this morning. Then I go below deck to put on the rice for dinner. Maggie and Mac stay on deck to tie up the sails and coil ropes.

In the galley, I turn on the cooker, like Mac showed me, and fill a saucepan with water. As it heats, I go over to my bag and pull out my phone. Sailing offshore, we wouldn't have great reception a lot of the time, Mac had explained, so I'd stowed my phone away. Now, when I switch it on, I receive a voicemail notification. I recognise Adam's number instantly.

Mac and Maggie come down the hatch into the body of the boat.

'You okay, Oli?' Mac asks. 'You look like you've seen a ghost.'

'I'm fine,' I manage, then tell them I'm just going upstairs to listen to a message.

On deck, lights from the city are scattered across the bay. The sky is stained at the edges by the glow of an industrial area. I make my way up to the bow of the boat, then sit down on a folded sail, cross-legged.

With trembling hands I dial my voicemail and hold the phone to my ear.

'*Liv, it's me,*' Adam says, his voice cracking. '*I've been thinking about everything. In fact, it's all I can think about.* You're *all I can think about.*' His voice cracks again, and he starts to sob. '*Fuck's sake.*' He coughs, clears his throat. '*I want you back. This is killing me. I'm sorry, okay? I'll be better. I'll do anything you want.*' He pauses, there's a sound in the background that I can't quite make out. '*I love you, okay? I love you.*'

I listen to the voicemail twice over, then Mac sticks his head through the hatch and calls out to me. 'You alright, kid?'

'Fine,' I say, wiping my eyes in the shadow of the mast.

'Dinner's ready.'

'Coming!'

I climb down the hatch and take my seat at the table. If Mac has noticed I've been crying, he doesn't say anything. Instead, he suggests we do a little reading after dinner.

I say, 'I'd love to, but I'm exhausted.'

'You sure you're okay, Oli?' says Maggie.

'Yeah,' I say. 'Promise.'

'Because you can talk to us about anything, alright? Nothing is a secret on a boat.'

I help clean up, then excuse myself for bed. I have a cabin all to myself under the cockpit. The ceiling is low, but I can see the moon through a porthole.

As I climb into bed, the *Sea Rose* rocks back and forth, gently, like a lullaby. I replay Adam's message in my head over and over.

I think of the first time he said it: *I love you.* How drunk he was. How amazing it had made me feel. He'd said it in front of Henry, and as he got up to go to the bar, I'd looked across at Henry and said, *Did you hear that?* Just to make sure it was real. Henry had smiled and nodded. It was real. Adam loved me. *Cool* Adam. The guy who commanded a room like gravity. Loved *me.*

I'd felt, in one breath, both whole and utterly breakable.

And then I think of when I first met Adam, walking into the lecture theatre at Sydney University, holding my books to my chest as a sea of eyes opened like flowers onto me. I remember the feeling that everyone already seemed to know each other. That feeling of loneliness only a crowd of strangers can give you. How his voice had cut through all the noise. *Hey, do you want to sit here?*

I remember how inviting his open arm had been. How, after that, everything else seemed to fall into place. How easily he'd brought me into his world. He made this new city feel exhilarating, because he had friends and a family who took me in, with all their parties and holidays. He gave me flowers on our one-month anniversary, and presents on my birthday. And he had still and quiet moments in which he said beautiful things that only I could hear.

But that's nostalgia. Filtering out the bad bits.

Because on our second night at sea, when we anchor by Broughton Island, there's another voicemail, in which Adam tells me I'm a whore, and that I've made the worst decision of my life. Shouting down the phone, he tells me I'll regret it, because I'm nothing without him. He says that all my friends are his friends and now they'll want nothing to do with me. And he's right.

Except that when I turn my phone off and go back up into the cockpit, tears pouring down my cheeks, Mac takes me in his arms and sits me down between him and Maggie. They wrap themselves around me, like rings of a tree, layer upon layer. So that I no longer feel exposed. I feel whole and, because their love doesn't make me weak, I feel unbreakable.

sea frangipani

I wake in the morning to the sound of a man right above my cabin, speaking loudly on the phone. I can't hear Maggie or Mac up there, so I pull on my jumper and a pair of leggings and go up on deck to check it out. But when I come out into the cockpit, I find there's no one except for me. Yet I can still hear the man, chatting away.

And then I see him, standing on a boat on the other side of the bay. It's so quiet his voice carries across the water so clearly it's as if he's standing right next to me.

Mac appears through the hatch in his board shorts. He walks past me up to the bow of the boat, climbs up onto the rail. Stands tall. Falls forward, pushing off at the last moment. His body arches in a perfect swan dive, barely making a splash. When he surfaces, he has a smile stretching from ear to ear. 'Ah,' he says, floating on his back. 'This is *living*!'

Over breakfast, Maggie asks me to read her a poem by H.D.

I read her 'Moonrise', finishing on:

She is great,

we measure her by the pine-trees.

'I love the line "*we have a song*".' Maggie smiles. 'Women are all kinds of unheard songs.'

Mac passes me a cup of orange juice. I take a sip as Maggie tells me about the first all-woman show she curated in London. 'It was one of the first London had ever seen. Hardly anyone came. But that didn't matter to me. I'd never been so proud of a show.'

'But if you were proud of it, surely you'd want people to see?'

'You're right,' she says. 'But what was important was that *I* saw those women. And they saw each other . . . Because even as women, we don't always see each other.'

'Did you keep putting on shows of women artists?'

'Of course.'

'Even though nobody came?'

'Those early shows asked, are we *women* artists? Or are we just artists, asserting ourselves, unapologetically?'

'Does it matter what we call ourselves?' I say.

'How can it *not*? We make our worlds with words.'

Mac comes on deck with a fishing rod. 'I think we need to add a new rule: twenty points for catching a fish,' says Mac.

'I thought you were a vegetarian,' I say.

'We eat fish if we catch them ourselves,' Maggie explains.

'Except salmon,' says Mac.

I cross my arms. 'Why not salmon?'

'They're monogamists. I respect that.'

Maggie laughs. 'I'd eat a salmon.'

'Yes, well, you're a heartbreaker, aren't you?'

Maggie blows a kiss in his direction.

'Do you believe in soulmates?' I ask.

Mac nods.

Maggie shakes her head. 'I do believe you can meet someone and feel like you've come home. But for me, love has always been plural.'

'Meaning?'

'Meaning I've loved and been loved by many people.'

I think of Adam, the good feelings intermingling with the bad. Pain and pleasure. The blue equilibrium. And I say, 'I'd be happy never to be in love again.'

Maggie makes a *hmm* sound, and then says, 'Tell me about that?'

'I just think . . .' I pause. How do I explain a grief that is so intricately intertwined with relief? 'I don't know . . . Like, one minute I feel fine, and the next I feel totally empty.'

She asks, 'How long were you with this person?'

'Four years.'

'That's a huge part of your life, then. Especially at your age.'

I try to summon memories of Sydney that don't involve Adam. But he's there, undulating through them all.

'My first love whittled me down,' says Maggie. 'God, it was a long time ago. But I can remember exactly how I felt.' She takes a deep breath. Exhales. 'I felt like he'd carved out parts of me, so slowly I didn't even realise what he was doing.'

My eyes glass over, blurring the horizon.

'And,' Maggie says, 'it wasn't until much later that I realised my first love wasn't really love at all.'

But I *loved* Adam, I think.

'Oli, have you ever seen how a forest grows back after a fire? How the leaves sprout from everywhere, even the trunks?'

'Yeah,' I say, though I'm not really following.

'Well, I think that's what love is supposed to be.'

A second later, there's a twang, a slackening, a giant pull. 'Oh, oh!' I shout. 'The line! We got a fish!'

Mac reels the line in, landing a fish in the cockpit. It's silver with blue stripes, iridescent in the sunlight. Mac calls for me to hold the fish. I lean down to stop it floundering as Mac reaches under his seat in the cockpit and pulls out a bottle of rum. He unscrews the lid, covers the fish's head with his hand and splashes alcohol on its gills. The fish goes limp instantly. He puts the rum back and pulls out a knife.

'Thank you,' he whispers to the fish, and then begins to slice. I look away. 'Oli,' he says, 'if you can't stomach the truth of killing the fish, you don't deserve to eat it.'

We have mackerel sashimi for dinner, anchored for the night in Port Macquarie. Afterwards, I climb into my bunk with bruised shins and stubbed toes, and a comment Maggie made swirling about behind my eyelids. Something about eating fish fresh from the ocean. A part of the ocean becoming a part of you.

In the morning, while we're eating breakfast, Mac says to me, 'It's time for you to rack up some of those distance points.'

We raise the anchor and motor out of the bay into open ocean, where a breeze is picking up. The sky is clouds layered like fish scales, fanning out.

'It's a mackerel sky,' Mac says, gazing up. 'This is good luck for a sailor, because it means it's about to get really windy.'

He sits me down at the helm. 'You've driven a car, right?'

I nod. 'Yeah.'

'Well, this might seem obvious, but it steers the same way as a car. Left is left. Right is right.'

'Don't you mean port is port, and starboard is starboard?'

Mac glances across at Maggie, who chuckles and says, 'Oh, she's good, isn't she!'

'Yeah, yeah. Well, the difference is, a road is fixed. It doesn't move. So you can read what the road is going to do to the car, because you can see the road ahead. The ocean, on the other hand, is always moving, so you have to read it as you are moving over it. More importantly, the ocean will talk to the boat, and the boat will react to what it hears. Your job is to listen to that conversation, and guide the boat to where you want it to go.' He takes my hand, puts it on the wheel, resting his hand lightly on top of mine. 'But you must coax it, steering it *just* enough . . . Using too much rudder is like shouting at the boat. You must be firm, confident, yet guide it gently.'

Mac lets go of my hand and sits down opposite me in the cockpit, next to Maggie.

I feel the *Sea Rose* lurch, straining against my hand on the wheel.

'Gently,' he says.

I soften my grip, feel the boat surf down the back of a swell.

'Now hold tight.'

I clutch the wheel, steering the boat up the oncoming wave.

Maggie cheers. 'Bravo!'

'You'll become familiar with the song of the ocean,' says Mac. 'Her lilting lullabies, her roaring . . . somethings!' He laughs. 'Can't think of the right word.'

'And if it all becomes too much, just close your eyes,' Maggie says. 'It makes it easier to hear.'

sea hibiscus

I'm coming up slowly, into the night. The deck is wet black, waves washing over the bow in this growing swell. The air is warm and thick. We're nearing the tropics now. I'm barefoot, wearing wet-weather pants, a singlet and a wet-weather jacket, unzipped in this heat. My hair is damp, my hands clammy. Trembling, just a little.

Mac is at the helm. He pats the seat beside him. I sit down. And he smiles. 'You're ready,' he says, gives me a hug, stands and shuffles across the cockpit towards the hatch, turning at the last moment to say, 'See you in four hours.' And then he disappears below deck.

Darkness encircles the boat. The moon and the stars are hidden behind a thick blanket of cloud. The only light comes from the glow of the navigation instruments. Sea spray is lit pink. Beyond it, the world is impossibly black. Like an Yves Klein monochrome, the sky is everything and nothing. Because no matter how close up and palpable this blackness is, it is at once unfathomably deep.

And so I sit here, in this strange, rosy haze, one hand on the boat, the other on the wheel, gripping so tight my knuckles turn white, because I feel now, with the sea indistinguishable from the sky, that if I let go of the boat I'll be sucked out into blackness. Like falling water. Into the abyss. Into everything. Into nothing.

At first I think my eyes are playing tricks on me as a thin band of orange stretches itself across the horizon port side.

Minutes grate. My pulse quickens.

The orange band grows thicker, becomes wider, until I see the colour take shape. The orange comes alive. It's moving, bending, dancing in the night.

I squint and the orange pulls into focus. I gasp.

Flames. They're flames!

The ocean is on fire. Is it an oil slick?

My hands are shaking now, my heart thumping. I fly through the cockpit and down the hatch to the nav station, where I flick on the desk lamp and pull up a chart.

'What is it?' I whisper aloud. Port side. It's land! We're close to the coast here, only a few miles offshore. I feel my heartbeat calming; it's not an oil slick.

I climb back up the ladder into the cockpit and walk up onto the port deck. Staring out, I can see it now. Tongues of fire. The land is burning.

I remember Mac pointing out a smear of grey in the sky this afternoon. 'We're in cane country now.' Here, he told me, farmers clear the land with fire.

I sit back down at the helm and breathe deep. Beyond me, embers take flight like moths swarming around the moon. It's terrifyingly beautiful.

Mac comes up on deck with two cups of tea as the sky opens into white, sea flowers opening their petals. Dawn is blooming. A beam of sunlight cuts across the horizon. Mac passes me my tea.

'How'd you sleep?' I ask.

'Like a baby,' he says, smiling widely. 'You survived your first night on watch.' He pats me on the back. 'I'm proud of you, kid.'

I take a sip of tea, feel it warming me up from the inside out.

Beyond the bow, the water is deep navy turning into something else. I watch in awe as the hours peel away; the sea becomes the blue of summer evenings, the blue of the number four, the blue of birdsong. It's brilliant and bold.

Mac is beaming. 'The Coral Sea,' he says. 'We're here.'

For lunch we have tinned spaghetti and warm bread. Maggie tells me that after five days at sea, *anything* tastes good. She's right. We've been at sea for almost two weeks, and I'm positive this is the best spaghetti I've ever had.

Afterwards, I wet a cloth with water from the sink and wipe the salt off my face. I've learnt that the more salt you get off, the easier it is to sleep.

I get into my bunk, having also learnt that, at sea, you sleep when you're able to. If you don't, you forget how to tie knots.

When I wake in the late afternoon, I find a packet of banana-flavoured lollies in my rucksack that I'd packed and forgotten about. I bring them on deck, sit down in the cockpit, stick one in my mouth and then offer the packet to Mac.

'What are these?'

'Banana lollies.'

He pulls back. 'Throw them overboard.'

'What?'

'Bananas are bad luck at sea.'

'They're only banana-*flavoured*.'

'I don't care.'

'You can't be serious.'

'No wonder we've been beating up-wind for two weeks. You've had bananas on board!'

'There's no actual banana in them!'

'Oli, they're bad luck. Throw them overboard.'

Maggie chimes in, 'It's also bad luck to have women at sea. Are you going to throw us overboard too?'

Mac laughs. 'Maybe I should.'

'You'd be lost without us,' she says, a cheeky smile spreading.

I put another of the lollies in my mouth.

'Hey! I saw that, kid.'

I roll my eyes, spit the lolly over the side.

'And the rest.'

'Why are they bad luck?'

Maggie explains, 'Bananas make the food around them spoil faster.'

'Fine,' I say, emptying the packet into the sea.

A gust of wind rises off the ocean, fills the sail. We lift two knots on the speedometer.

'See?' Mac says. 'It's working already!'

Sitting next to Maggie, I whisper in her ear, 'I've still got another packet below deck.'

She cracks up, then whispers back, 'Save some for me.'

Islands come into focus the way you wake up on a Sunday morning: slowly, like a painting, layer by layer. Block blue, at first. Then daubs of green, the outlines of trees, a band of white sand. A brown slab takes shape, all wrinkled and folded rock, until the cliff face opens its eyes.

A day later, we anchor for lunch on an island fringed by coral. To get there, we have to weave between two coral shelves. We drop the sails and turn on the motor. Mac comes up from the nav station with a chart, spreads it across the cockpit. I'm at the helm, listening to him call the shots.

'Easy, easy,' he tells me. 'Slow down a notch.'

I pull back the gearstick at my feet, steer starboard. My eyes are on the depth instrument when, out of the corner of my eye, I spot a fin. I look across the port side to see a grey fin. 'A dolphin!' I exclaim, then see the grey body snake back under water. 'Oh my God, a shark!'

'Concentrate!' Mac shouts.

'I just saw a shark!'

'Do you want to run us aground?'

'Sorry,' I mutter.

'Now, hook port side,' he says, 'around this lump of coral.'

I steer the boat around a patch of rippled pink water.

'Now into reverse,' he instructs.

I flick the motor into reverse. The boat rocks on its heels, pulls back. Mac jumps up out of the cockpit and heads up to the bow. 'Neutral!' he calls out.

I put the motor in neutral, and he lowers the anchor.

'Very good! Now off, please!'

I turn the motor off, and listen. The island is alive with birdsong. A sea eagle takes flight, soars down the cliff face, spreads out across the water.

Mac jumps back into the cockpit. 'Time for a swim?'

'A swim?' I say. 'I just saw a shark!'

'Doubt it,' he says. 'It was probably a dolphin.'

'It wasn't swimming like a dolphin.'

Mac ignores me, goes down below with Maggie. They emerge minutes later wearing their swimmers. 'Come on, Oli,' Maggie says.

'No way,' I say.

'At least feel the water,' says Mac.

'Fine,' I say, edging towards the back of the cockpit. I grip the lifeline, slowly lowering one leg down to dip my toes in the water. But before I touch it, there are hands on my back, pushing me in. I fall forwards into the drink, fully dressed in my board shorts and singlet. My belly flop is spectacular.

I surface coughing and spluttering. Mac and Maggie are on deck, pissing themselves. I start swimming towards the ladder, panicked by something that touched my foot, but I must wait for Maggie who is already coming down into the water. She enters the sea the way you come home, dropping your keys on the table, breathing out. A sigh of relief, the way the ocean holds her.

Behind her, Mac jumps in, his splash coming over both of us.

And now I'm laughing too.

Back on deck, we have Vegemite on rye biscuits for lunch with peach fruit cups for dessert. I've just put a piece of peach in my mouth when I see a fin surface just beyond the stern, a grey body snaking through the water. I shriek, spitting the peach into my lap. 'Look! I told you!'

'Oh yeah, that's definitely a shark,' Mac says, and Maggie bursts into laughter.

'It's not funny!' I say. 'We could have been eaten!'

'They're only reef sharks, they won't eat you.'

'Yeah,' Maggie says. 'Maybe just a toe.'

I've been to Beijing, a city stacked into the sky. Bangkok, hot and heaving. New York, towering. Rome, ornate and opulent. Yet as I fix my snorkel to my face and dive beneath the surface, I realise no city I've ever seen compares to a city made of coral. It's vastly intricate. Infinitely complex. Schools of fish dart between swaying yellow seaweed. The seabed blooms like sea hibiscus. Starfish adorn rocks. Emperor angelfish glide through sun-lanced waters. I equalise my ears, swim deeper to where humphead wrasse move like gentle giants.

It's like walking through an art gallery. Walls of shells and barnacles are framed in gold leaf. Coral statues sit atop algae-covered plinths. Everywhere I look, everywhere I turn, a new work is unveiled. The sea, the finest curator.

But then I swim over a drop-off towards another shelf of coral and see only white, the pinks and purples leached from the coral like blood drained from a vein. The occasional fish swims between the bleached bones.

When I surface, the sunset is marbled on the water. I swim back over to the boat, climb up the ladder and find a towel in the cockpit. I wipe the salt off me. Maggie is already there, a towel wrapped around her body, her hair sleek silver.

'What did you think?' she asks.

I'm speechless.

'Beautiful, isn't it?'

'Yeah,' I say. 'But there's a patch where the coral is all white with hardly any fish. What happened to it?'

'Bleaching,' Mac says, climbing up the ladder. 'The worst the reef has ever seen last year.' He reaches for a towel. 'You can thank climate change for that. The ocean is warming, and it's becoming more acidic.'

I feel an uncomfortable weight in my stomach, wondering if Mac has told Maggie that my dad works in oil.

'You know,' Maggie says, 'I mourned losing my eyesight, but I'm almost relieved I can't see the reef now. It'd break my heart.'

Mac sighs. 'The Great Barrier Reef is the living dead.'

We anchor for the night in Blue Pearl Bay. Over dinner, Mac tells me there's a humphead wrasse living here called Priscilla. He says that when you dive under, you can hear her beak crunching on the reef.

'Soon,' Maggie says, 'you'll hear whale song.'

'Whale song?' I say. 'You're kidding.'

Maggie shakes her head. 'Honestly.'

'If there's a whale within ten miles, you can hear it when you stick your head under,' Mac says.

I laugh. 'You're pulling my leg.'

'Just you wait,' Maggie says.

Mac reaches into the cupboard above the sink. 'Dessert, anyone?'

'What have we got?' I ask.

'Apple puree pots,' Mac says, passing one to each of us.

As we eat, I think of our walk this morning across Whitsunday Island to Whitehaven Beach. The tangle of vines strung around the track. The blue soldier crabs scuttling at low tide. I picture the muddy spots that freckle manta ray wings in the shallows. Wispy grasses like fine green hair on sand dunes. Twisted branches and orange rocks. And then I close my eyes, and I imagine that wash of turquoise sea swathed around a curve of white sand.

'Today was a good day,' I say. 'Thank you so much for bringing me here.'

Maggie reaches out to me, touches my forearm, feels her way down to my hand resting on the table. She holds it. 'No,' she says. 'Thank *you*.'

'Psst,' Mac whispers, coaxing me out of darkness. 'Oli, wake up.'

I feel a hand on my shoulder. My eyes fly open.

'Sorry, kid, didn't mean to frighten you. But you gotta come see this.'

'What is it?' I mutter, rolling onto my side, propping myself up on one elbow.

'You'll see,' he says.

I wriggle out of my bunk and follow him through the cabin, up the stairs, through the hatch, into something else.

The ocean is glowing, iridescent. Like a silver muscle, pulsating. Ripples of dragonfly blue. Sways of rose gold.

I whisper, 'What is it?'

'Phosphorescence.'

I walk to the back of the cockpit and lean over the safety rail, looking down through black glass to the sea floor, everything illuminated. Rainbow fish scales sparkling like jewels in an underwater cave. This coral city, lit up like Atlantis. All glittering gold. Teeming. And endless.

And there is the feeling that I'm beyond myself. As if I'm gazing into outer space, watching a galaxy being born. I hold my breath as the universe takes shape in wrinkled corals. Blooms of pink algae flowering like a summer storm.

This underwater world.

All silver and pink. I watch it.

Becoming and unbecoming in a single pulse.

sea iris

There's light. Like headlights. Headlights on a truck, coming at me, coming for me. I wake in a burst. Gasp. Air rushes in. Hot air. I'm in the tropics. My eyes dart around the cabin. I'm in my bunk. On the *Sea Rose*. I'm okay.

But what *is* that light? I squint at the blinding white that's pushing through the porthole above my bunk. A floodlight, maybe. Pointed right at us.

I shuffle through the cabin, unlock the hatch door and climb up into the cockpit. I turn to face the light and my breath catches in my throat. It's not a light at all, just a reflection of one.

Never have I seen the moon so bright. I hold out my hand. I can see the lines across my palms, can make out the shape of my fingerprint. I look down at the deck, washed white. My moon shadow is stark, bold. Defiant.

And then I look up, my eyes slowly adjusting. Stars come into focus, spreading out across the sky like silver dust blown into shapes.

I go downstairs and grab my blanket and pillow from my bunk, bringing them up on deck. I lie down and gaze out, only there's no horizon to hold on to. There are only stars. Everywhere. Floating in space. Floating on the sea. Stars raining down, thousands of them. Like falling water. I catch them on my skin.

And it's silent. So silent.

I cough. I hear it. *Ears still working.*

But this silence . . . Lying here, grazing on stars. This silence is total.

Like I'm in the eye of the storm. The iris of the sea.

As the sky whitens, the islands wake with birdsong.

Melodies flow through the pines, cascade over cliffs, landing on the water where they swirl in wide blue circles. These islands are ancient, Maggie had told me last night between poems. They were once part of a mountain range. Bodies made of hoop pines and mammoth boulders. Not the tropical palms I'd dreamt of.

'If you hold your hand up and block out the view of the water,' Mac said, 'you'd almost believe you were standing on a bush track in a mountain forest, hundreds of miles from the sea.'

I sit up in the cockpit, cover the bay with my hand, and feel the years peel away. Slowly, slowly, and then all at once I am barefoot on brown earth, running through the pines, between shadows and marbled bark. Wooded children stretch their wings, singing songs that catch on the wind, funnelling through valleys.

A breeze touches my cheek, as if the island is reaching out to me through its ringed wood, layer by layer, century by century. I lower my hand and see a turtle come up for breath, its head like wet stone. I rush to the back of the cockpit to watch it dive beneath the surface. The water is so clear; I follow it, deeper and deeper, as it glides between bulbs of coral.

'You're up early,' a voice says behind me. I turn around and Mac passes me a cup of tea. He eyes the blanket and pillow in the cockpit. 'Sleep up here, did ya?'

I take a sip of tea, nodding.

'Pretty special, isn't it?'

I nod because there's no sound in me to describe the thrill of no sound.

Later, Maggie lowers herself down the ladder into the sea. Mac dives in behind her. I jump in, tucked into a ball. When I come up, Mac is coughing on sea water. 'Cheeky,' he says, splashing me. I laugh and dive down again. Holding my nose to stop my breath escaping, I hang underwater and listen to the reef crackling. The sounds of the beaks crunching and bubbles popping appear behind my eyelids in bursts of yellow and pink.

I surface, breathe in deep. The morning air tastes of salt and dark wood.

Maggie climbs back up the ladder. Mac asks if I want to swim to shore.

'Sure!' I call out, and start kicking towards the beach. As I swim, I open my eyes underwater. The corals beneath blur together like splotches of paint on a palette.

Each time I come up for breath, the hoop pines become more pronounced, their outlines sharper, their immensity more overwhelming, until I am standing in the shallows, gazing up at the towering trees. Wooded bodies stand one after another, like the mountainside is an amphitheatre for a green choir singing all kinds of unheard songs.

I walk out of the water onto centuries of crushed seashells. Pieces of bone coral mark the high-tide line. My footprints dance between the scuttle marks of crabs, all the way up to the first pine at the foot of the forest. I reach out to touch the bark, and imagine for a moment that I can feel the vibrations of its song.

She is great,
We measure her by the pine-trees.

Back on board, Mac points to the top of the mast and says, 'The main halyard and spinnaker halyard are tangled. How are you with heights?'

'Ugh,' I say. 'Okay?'

'Good,' he says, winking. 'Let's get you harnessed up.'

'Hang on . . . *What?*'

But he doesn't hear me. He's already down the hatch, returning a minute later with a harness. I'm wearing a bikini top and board shorts. Mac tells me to put a t-shirt on so the harness doesn't chafe my stomach.

I grab a t-shirt, come up on deck and, before I can think twice, I'm in the harness being hoisted up the mast.

'How tall is the mast?' I shout.

'Doesn't matter!' Mac calls back.

Maggie is in the cockpit. 'You're almost there!'

'You don't know that!' I scream, and she chuckles.

When I get to the top of the mast, my palms are clammy. Mac calls out something about looping a red rope under a blue rope. I try to detangle the red from the blue, but my hands are shaking and I can't get a decent grip.

'You got it?' he shouts.

'Give me a minute!'

'Take your time.'

I look down at Mac and Maggie, their bodies shrunk to toy figurines from this height. I take a deep breath, exhale, and let go of the ropes, sitting back in my harness. I let go of the mast and let myself hang there, smiling the way you might if you were looking down at your family portrait—the one that had to be retaken because everyone was laughing.

My nerves begin to calm. And soon, I'm untangling the ropes, feeling a thrill in solving this problem for Mac and Maggie. Like I'm part of this boat. This body. This family.

The sun is setting when Maggie suggests one more swim before dinner.

'Well, I'm already in my swimmers,' I say.

I dive off the bow into water as warm as a bath. I remember the story Pa used to tell about the sun living in the sea. There is a pinch felt deep inside me, a pain in my heart, as I recall how much I'd loved that story, how different he'd been when Nan was still alive. I like to think they're together now, flowing through the earth in a river, deep underground. I smile, and swim around to the stern where Maggie is descending the ladder. She dives under, surfacing a moment later with her mouth gaping.

'Oli, Oli! Whale song!' she shouts, before diving under again.

I exhale, close my eyes and sink down beneath the surface. I drift there, a moment, and then I hear it.

I hear whale song in swirls of violet and Prussian blue.

And in the same way that realising the blue of the sky is only an illusion marks both the death of innocence and the birth of imagination, listening to whale song is both an ending and a beginning. It's the lifting of a veil.

And there's the feeling of history happening all at once. Like I've been here before, my body dreamt in swirls of violet and Prussian blue. Like I'm coming home, finally.

sea monsters

fish bone

The air in the tropics is dense heat. I walk through a garden of palm fronds, into a yacht club. I wipe my upper lip on the back of my hand, slick my hair back into a ponytail. My eyes are slowly adjusting to the shadows.

The yacht club is carpeted, a chequered pattern of bright yellow and blue squares that makes me think I've stepped back in time three decades. My sandals stick to the damp carpet. It smells of beer and salt and Chapstick.

I make my way over to the bar, where a woman is pouring beers for two men with burnt necks.

'Ah,' one man says after taking a sip, 'that's better.'

He clinks his glass against his friend's. 'Cheers, mate.'

'Cheers.'

The woman turns to face me. '*Bonjour*,' she says.

'Sorry,' I say. 'English?'

She nods. 'What can I get for you?'

'Actually, I'm looking for someone. A guy named Vlad. Do you know him?'

'Yes,' she says, scanning the bar. 'Over there.' She points to a man sitting out on the deck with a beer and a cigarette, a spiral of smoke curling in the afternoon sun.

'*Merci*,' I say.

'You're welcome.'

I walk out onto the deck and move to stand in front of him, casting a shadow across his broad chest.

'Vlad?'

He eyes me suspiciously. 'Yeah?'

'I'm Olivia.'

Vlad shades his eyes with his hand. Squinting, he looks me up and down. 'Have we met?'

'No. Well, kind of. You emailed me.'

He stubs out his cigarette, frowns. 'Did I?'

'You're skippering *Poseidon*, aren't you?'

'Yeah.'

'You emailed me about the NZ delivery.'

He opens his mouth to speak. Hesitates. 'What'd you say your name is?'

'Olivia.' I think of the email I sent and remember how I'd signed off. 'Oli?'

'Oh!' Vlad cracks up.

I shift my weight from one leg to the other. The couple on the table across the deck look over to us, at this man laughing, at me, silent.

'Sorry, sorry,' he says at last. 'You're just not what I expected.'

I cross my arms. 'What were you expecting?'

'A lad.'

'Ah, right . . .'

He kicks out the chair opposite him, motions with his hand for me to take it. I sit down, cross my legs.

'Want a drink?' he asks.

'Nah, I'm good. Thanks.'

He takes a sip of his beer. 'You've been to sea, yeah?'

'What?'

His arms protrude from his tank top, pink and meaty. His eyes are pointed, like shards of blue ice.

'I've been working on boats for four years,' I say. 'I thought I told you that in the email?'

Vlad leans forwards in his chair, puts both elbows on the table. And suddenly this is starting to feel like an interview. Like I don't already have the job. He takes another sip of his beer.

'Yeah, cool. It's just that I'm skippering four guys. I thought it was gonna be five.'

'I know how to pull my weight.'

'Have you ever been at sea with a crew of all lads?'

I shake my head. A strange heat is crawling across my skin.

He pulls a cigarette from the deck on the table, offers the pack to me. I go to take one then reconsider. Pretending to smoke would surely be worse than passing up the offer. Vlad sparks his cigarette. Inhales, exhales. Takes another sip of his beer.

'How good are you in a galley?'

The fucking kitchen? I feel my mouth drop open. But before any sound escapes, another guy appears. He claps Vlad on the back then pulls a seat over from the table beside us. 'Am I interrupting?' he asks as he joins us.

Vlad shakes his head, and the new guy offers me his hand.

'I'm Cam,' he says. His eyes are deep brown.

I shake his hand. 'Olivia,' I say.

He squeezes my hand. And I notice his nose is a little bent, perhaps broken once, the crookedness oddly endearing.

Vlad butts in. 'Oli,' he says. '*This* is Oli.'

'Ha!' Cam laughs. 'No shit! *You* are not what I expected.'

'So I've heard,' I say, letting go of his hand.

Vlad draws on his cigarette, blows smoke across the table.

'It's a nice surprise, though,' Cam says, and Vlad rolls his eyes.

I feel myself blushing. That strange heat is twisting around my waist.

Vlad shrugs, then mutters, 'It's bad luck to have a chick at sea.'

'I worked the galley on my last two deliveries,' I lie, having never, in four years, worked a delivery where we didn't *share* the kitchen duties. But I can feel this job slipping through my fingers, and I've been hanging around the docks in Noumea for weeks now, waiting to join a crew. I think of my bank account. Barely enough money for a few more nights in the hostel.

'I know how to cook,' I insist.

Cam grins. 'You've got my vote.' Then he turns to Vlad. 'Come on, mate,' he says, prodding Vlad's arm. 'Not afraid of a silly superstition, are you?'

Vlad laughs. The sound is hollow pink.

The day is just peeling open when I leave my hostel for the dock. I've got my life in a rucksack slung over my shoulder. Clothes, my passport, a purse with coins in several currencies, some toiletries, sailing gloves, wet-weather gear, a handful of letters from Maggie and Mac, and my own copy of *A Field Guide to Getting Lost*, which they sent me for my last birthday.

On the way to the yacht club, I pass through a local market. Among the wild fruits are a line of sarongs, swaying in a yellow breeze. There's a table of jewellery made from seashells. Fish, skinned and filleted. Cracked coconuts served with plastic straws. And paintings. I pause a moment to gaze at an artist's impression of the reef as seen from above. Tendrils of turquoise. Blooms of coral like pale blue birthmarks. And my mind falls back two years to a delivery I worked in Indonesia. Diving off the coast of Lombok. Eating freshly caught fish on deck.

Then I think of the week I spent between jobs on the island of Bali. Sipping Balinese coffee in a warung, a fan clicking overhead. I think of the waterfalls in the mountains, nestled between lush jungle. How the water came over me in a rush of cold white. And then I think of the art, of the paintings that crowded marketplaces. How I'd had the privilege of entering one man's studio, watching Bali take shape in daubs of paint. How it had changed the way I read the landscape. Like land coming into focus, I noticed *everything.* The carved edges of houses and backyard temples. Smoky offerings of flowers and rice. Streets lined with towering poles made from dried palm fronds and fabric for Galungan festival. How I'd written to Maggie and Mac about all these wild colours I'd never felt before.

My stomach rumbles, drawing me back to this day in this marketplace. I search my rucksack for my wallet, and with the last of my money I buy watermelon juice and a banana, eating and drinking as I walk.

I find Cam by the front door of the yacht club. He smiles when he sees me. 'How ya going?' he asks, giving me a hug.

I shrug. 'Fine. A bit tired.'

'Well, you look great,' he says.

'Thanks,' I mutter, yawning.

Cam suggests that I don't yawn like that in front of the guys. 'Everyone takes watches in Vlad's crew, even if you're working the galley.'

I nod, closing my mouth, sealing it shut.

He opens the door for me, gently touching the curve of my back as I step through.

Poseidon is tied up in the last row of berths. Her hull is painted scarlet, a full-bodied red. Like puckered lips. A lobster tail.

There are three guys on deck. Vlad is standing at the bow. Two others are in the cockpit.

Someone whistles. The way someone might whistle out of a car. At a woman.

I look up to where the sound came from to see a guy slung in a harness at the top of the mast. 'Hey!' he calls out, waving.

'That's Ajax—call him AJ,' says Cam, pointing to him.

I smile and wave back.

At the stern of the boat, Cam introduces me to Hunter and Zach.

I shake their hands. 'Nice to meet you.'

'Yeah, you too,' says Zach.

Hunter smiles. 'You ready for a week with these idiots?'

Zach says, 'Speak for yourself, dude.'

I laugh. 'As ready as I'll ever be.'

'Where ya from?' Hunter asks me. 'Can't pick your accent.'

I think of each time I arrived at a new school growing up, how many times I was asked this question. *Themyscira*, I used to say.

That's not a real place, the other kids would respond.

Yes it is.

Is not.

The most powerful women in the world live there.

You're making it up. There's no such place.

I look at Hunter, standing bare-chested in a pair of washed-out board shorts. 'Australia,' I say. 'Originally. But I grew up in Asia—Hong Kong mostly.'

'Why?'

'Dad's work.'

'Must have been cool.'

I shrug. 'Yeah, it was pretty good.'

'Vlad's a pom,' he says. 'Zach is from Cali and Cam is a Kiwi. But don't you worry.' He winks. 'I've got your back. I'm an Aussie. From Perth.'

Behind us, Zach is lowering AJ down the mast. When AJ gets to the bottom, he unhooks his carabiner and jumps down into the cockpit. Still wearing the harness, he's bulging between the straps. AJ looks at me, a smile brewing. He offers his hand to shake, but when I take it he turns it over and kisses the top of my hand. '*Enchanté*,' he says.

Hunter rolls his eyes.

'Are you French?' I ask.

'My mum is, yes.'

'Well, it's nice to meet you too,' I say, my cheeks warming.

He wriggles out of the harness and puts it under the bench seat in the cockpit. Then, standing up straight, he turns back to me. He's striking, with silky green eyes, a shadow of stubble and a shock of volcanic black hair. He takes off his t-shirt, uses it to wipe the sweat off his forehead. 'Yes,' he says. 'What a pleasure.'

Vlad steps down into the cockpit. 'There's a northerly blowing until tomorrow afternoon. I want to catch the best of it, okay, boys?' He turns to me. 'Let's get you familiar with the boat so we can leave before lunch.'

At sea, land fades like a watercolour left out in the rain, the details bleeding together until the mountains wash into paper sky. And then it is all sea. Here. There. Everywhere. Like the boat has become its own little world. A red planet, drifting through blue.

I draw a deep breath, feeling myself open out into the void.

This is the moment I relish most every time: leaving land, when the near and the far fold into each other. It's a returning. Home.

For our first night at sea, I boil potatoes and mash them with mixed herbs, garlic, butter, salt, pepper and mustard. For a side, I steam vegies with lemon and salt.

The yacht is the biggest I've worked on, fifty-eight feet, but it's a racing yacht, so its interior is sparse. Comforts are sacrificed for speed efficiency. There's a single cabin at the bow, with a bed doubling as storage for sails. Beside it is a toilet with a door that won't latch. In the middle of the main cabin are two rows of bunk beds—slings hanging from the walls. Then there's the galley, where my carrots and broccoli are softening, and the nav station, where Vlad is charting our course. Behind, at the back of the boat, the space under the cockpit is storage for more sails.

There are no walls to divide sleep from work from eat. No walls to get changed behind. On a yacht, I've learnt, nothing is discreet. On *this* yacht, red sky is wide open. Everything is on show.

I give Vlad his meal at the nav station. I want to ask him about the course he's plotting, but there's something in the hunch of his shoulders, in the terse way he says, 'Thanks,' without looking up, that I find intimidating. He's only a few years older than me, yet he makes me nervous in a way a skipper never has before. I feel his words, *bad luck*, looming. Like a roll cloud. And so I refrain from asking a question he might find stupid.

I take dinner on deck for the rest of the guys. Zach is at the helm, steering. He's wearing board shorts and a linen shirt, unbuttoned, the fabric flapping at the edges. He's clean-shaven with a sun-kissed crew cut and a thin leather bracelet. His hard jawline makes him appear older than the rest of us, though we're all in our twenties.

Hunter, the youngest of the crew at only twenty-one, is sitting up on the side of the cockpit behind Zach. Though he has a head of messy curls, his body is hairless. He's skinny, his pale skin taut over lean muscle.

'You got burnt today,' I say as I hand him his plate.

Hunter eyes his pink shoulders, laughs. 'Sorry, *Mum*.'

I give Cam and AJ their dinners, then go down below to fetch mine. When I come back on deck, AJ slides along the bench seat to make room for me between him and Cam. I sit down and both guys edge a little closer.

'This is delicious,' AJ says.

Cam adds, 'I knew you were a good decision.'

I eat a mouthful of potato, feel it thick in my throat. It's hard to swallow.

Vlad enters the cockpit a moment later, his strawberry blond hair shining in the late sun. He has his dinner in one hand and a small whiteboard in the other. He sits down, puts his plate at his feet, and rests the whiteboard on his knee. He pulls a marker from his shorts pocket.

'Two-and-a-half-hour watches,' he says, 'starting from eight.'

Five sailors, two-and-a-half-hour watches from eight. I do the maths. Someone is getting a full night's sleep.

'I'll take first watch,' he says, writing his name in the first slot on the whiteboard. 'And then Hunter, you can do ten thirty to one. Zach, you're one to three thirty.' He looks up at me, Cam, AJ. 'Which of you wants the darkest hour?'

Cam shrugs. 'I don't mind.'

'Okay, then,' says Vlad. 'You're three thirty to six. And AJ can take sunrise, six to eight thirty.'

'What about Oli?' asks Hunter.

'She can go on with Cam.'

'If I go on watch by myself,' I say, 'we'll have shorter watches.'

'Exactly,' says Hunter.

'I think that until we've all sailed together,' says Vlad, 'it's a good idea to double up.'

I feel that strange heat crawling up my neck.

Zach says, 'At least for the first night.'

'I agree,' says Cam. 'Better safe than sorry.'

I wake to a hand on my shoulder. 'Oli, time for watch.'

I climb out of my bunk. Moonlight exposes my naked thighs. I step aside, hiding myself in the shadows as I search my bunk for my shorts. Finding them at the foot of the bunk, I quickly step into them. Cam passes me my wet-weather jacket. I wait until I'm through the hatch and in the cockpit to put it on. The heat below deck is meaty.

'How'd you sleep?' he asks.

I think of the hour's sleep I lost cleaning up after dinner. And the snoring that had already started by the time I finally got into my bunk. I'd lain there for hours, trying to imagine the snoring as a thunderstorm rolling through the bunk above me.

'Fine,' I say.

'Good,' he says. 'Me too.'

I sit down at the helm. I'm barefoot, with my jacket unzipped. The sea breeze drifting around my torso is a welcome reprieve. I inhale it deep into my lungs. Feel the sky coursing through me.

The moon tonight is a sliver, like a cat's eye. The paleness of it opens up the night to a swathe of stars. They ripple through the black like a river twisting overhead.

'Wow,' says Cam, looking up. 'I forgot about *this*.'

'Forgot?' I ask.

'It's been a while since my last delivery,' he says.

And *I'm* the one who isn't trusted with a solo watch.

'Pretty incredible,' I say, gazing across a pool of stars.

'I'm not religious or anything,' he says, 'but out here, it's kinda hard to believe there isn't a God. Don't you think?'

I shrug, casting my mind back to a conversation with Mac and Maggie in another time, on another sea. We'd been talking about my pa.

'You'll see him again,' Maggie had said.

I shook my head. 'I don't believe in heaven.'

'That's not what I meant,' she told me. 'There are other ways of seeing, Oli. I see wind in shades of red. I see Mac laughing in green.' She hesitated. 'And I see Robynne in a breeze filling the sails pink.'

Across the cockpit, Mac closed his eyes and I watched his body soften, his lips just hinting at a smile.

'You okay?' asks Cam, drawing me back into *this* time, on *this* sea. A breeze rises from the water. A woman's body fills the sails.

'Yeah. I was just thinking of something a friend told me.'

'Gotta concentrate when you're on watch,' he says.

'I know.'

'Sorry, I'm not trying to tell you what to do or anything.'

I cross my arms.

'When I first started, I'd drift off too sometimes,' he says. 'You've just gotta be careful of that—that's all I'm trying to say.'

'This isn't my first watch.'

'What?'

'I've been working on boats for four years.'

'How old are you?'

'Twenty-five.'

'Oh, no shit.' He laughs. 'You're the same age as me.'

I look over his shoulder to check the nav instruments.

'Sorry,' he says, 'you just don't look your age.'

'Thanks?'

'Nah, I just mean, like, you're really hot.'

For breakfast, I slice papaya and watermelon into cubes, and put them in a big bowl in the middle of the cockpit. Everyone is up except for AJ, who's sleeping after his early watch.

Back in the galley I boil five eggs, let them cool in cold water, and then take them up on deck, pass them around. When I give Cam his, he grins. 'Thanks, babe.'

Hunter is peeing over the back of the boat. He shakes himself in the wind, then tucks back into his board shorts and turns to take the boiled egg off me.

'Eugh,' I say, laughing. 'Wash your hands first.'

He rolls his eyes, sticks his hands over the stern deck, reaching into the ocean. Turning back to me, he smirks and flicks his hands so water flies off them onto my skin.

I shriek, stumble backwards, trip over a coil of rope and fall back. Hard.

I land at an angle on the winch, my torso bending in a way torsos aren't meant to bend, and something inside me cracks.

I feel the crack in a piercing purple.

There is laughter around me, but the shock of pain distorts the sound; it ripples around me as if I'm deep underwater. The sky and sea blur together. I can't breathe. Pain shoots out from my rib in waves. Electric. Hot. My side is on fire. I roll onto my back, my eyes squeezed shut.

'Are you okay?'

I can't breathe. I can't *breathe.*

'Shut up. I think she's hurt.'

'Oli, are you okay?'

'Where does it hurt?'

'Help her up.'

Hands scoop behind my shoulders. Hands hoist me to my feet. But my legs don't work. They quake, give way, and I collapse into someone else's arms. His arms.

Hands hold me straight. Hands touch my side, my rib. I cry out in pain. And then I'm throwing up. Only there's nothing in my stomach. Just water and bile. It lands on someone's feet.

'Gross!'

'Shut the fuck up.'

'Oli?'

'Take her below deck.'

In my bunk, my breaths are shallow. Every inhale is piercing purple.

I can hear voices at the nav station.

'We have to go back.'

'We can't.'

'I really think—'

'She'll be fine.'

'She's hurt!'

'I think it's serious.'

'It's just a bad bruise.'

'She's a girl.'

'Probably tired after watch.'

'Just needs to sleep.'

A voice whispers in my ear. 'Oli?'

I open one eye.

'Can you sit up? I've got painkillers.'

Cam helps me to sit up in my bunk.

'Here,' he says, putting two pills in my mouth. 'Drink this.' He offers me a cup of water.

I take a swig, swallowing the pills.

He helps me to lie back down. I reach for his arm, wrap my hand around his wrist.

'We're going back, yeah?' I manage between sharp breaths.

'Yep,' he says, patting me on the shoulder. 'See if you can get some rest.'

I wake in a cold sweat. The light in the cabin is dim. Out a porthole, I see the sun is setting. I can hear voices up on deck. I need to pee.

I struggle out of the bunk, stumble through the shadows to the toilet. The latch is broken, so the door swings open and close on its hinges, slamming with each rise and fall of the swell. I feel each slam resound through my body.

After I flush, I fumble my way back through the cabin to the nav station, where I get up the electronic chart to see how far we are from Noumea.

I gasp.

The sudden breath sends a hot wave of pain through my body.

'Fucking arseholes,' I mutter, collapsing back into the chair.

That strange heat, snaking up my back, wrapping around my neck.

I stare at the screen, where *Poseidon* is a tiny blip in a chasm of blue. Pushing o n t o w a r d s N e w Z e a l a n d .

fish eye

The sky is dusty when another boat appears on the electric chart. It's dark by the time we see the boat's lights on the horizon. Like tiny red and green stars.

'Do you know the rule about passing another boat?' Zach asks me.

Hunter butts in, 'When red and green you see in front, full steam ahead and ram the cunt.'

I roll my eyes. 'You steer starboard,' I say. But beneath their laughter, no one hears me.

I feel time pass in heartbeats. Each thump against my cracked rib. Piercing purple. Tick tock.

I'm making dinner for our third night at sea. Couscous and boiled vegetables. Vlad comes down the ladder as I'm serving it onto the plates. I drop a potato, bend to pick it up. Pain fans out from my rib, courses through my torso. I wince.

'That bad, is it?' he says. Though it doesn't feel like a question.

I stand straight, shudder. I want to throw up. 'I'm fine,' I say.

'Good,' he says, half smiling. He picks up two plates and takes them upstairs to the cockpit. I follow behind with another two and then return below deck for the rest.

The wind is dying around us as we eat. The sails slacken and begin to flap.

After dinner, Vlad, Cam and Zach gather around the nav station opposite the galley where I'm washing up. AJ comes down the ladder. 'Want some help?'

'Yeah, could you dry, please?'

'Of course,' he says, his dimples appearing when he smiles.

Over at the nav station, I hear Zach suggest we turn the motor on. Vlad says something about not wasting fuel unless we have to. I pass a plate to AJ, wipe my hands dry on my shorts and cross the cabin to the nav station.

'What if we sailed off course a little, like down here, and got the tail end of this storm cell?' I say, pointing south-west on the chart to the edge of a weather system that would promise stronger winds.

'That's completely in the wrong direction,' Zach objects.

'I know. But we're in dead water here.'

Zach mutters, 'Better here than *there*.'

'What?' I snap.

'I said, better here than all the way over there,' he says, waving his hand. 'We're going to New Zealand, remember?'

'Whatever,' I say, turning and walking back to the sink full of dishes.

When I pass the final plate to AJ, his hand touches mine. He holds it there a moment, his fingertips brushing my palm. He smiles. Those dimples.

'I liked your idea,' he whispers in my ear.

And I want to say, *Well, maybe you should say that,* and, *They actually listen to you*, and, *I like my idea too, because it's a fucking good idea.* But I don't say any of those things. Because the way his hand touches mine is a gentle glow in the shadows below deck, and I don't want that light to go out. So I just smile, pink-cheeked, and say, 'Thank you.'

Thump. Tick. Thump. Tock.

The boys decide not to change course. Instead they just tighten the sails and push on in three knots of breeze, despite the two knots of tide pushing against us. Three steps forward, two steps back. New Zealand is painfully far away. I feel the weight of the ocean beneath us. It's everywhere.

'I'm bored,' Hunter says, throwing his cards down on the table.

'You just can't handle losing,' says Cam.

'*No,* I just can't handle another round of this stupid game.'

'What else can we play?' I ask.

'How about "Never have I ever".'

'Never have I what?'

Hunter's eyes widen. 'You've never heard of "Never have I ever"?'

I shake my head.

Cam asks, 'How long did you say you'd worked on boats for?'

Zach laughs.

'We all start holding up three fingers, and we go around the circle and have to say something we've never done, and if someone else at the table has done it they have to put a finger down,' explains Hunter.

'And the loser is the first person to lose all their fingers?'

'Or the winner,' Hunter says, grinning. 'Usually you'd just have to finish your drink . . .'

'Well, we do have rum,' says Cam.

'That we do,' Hunter says with a cheeky smile.

'I don't think Vlad would agree to that,' says Zach.

'Why don't you ask him?' Hunter says.

'You ask him.'

'Fine.' Hunter gets up from the table and climbs the ladder into the cockpit where Vlad is sitting alone on watch.

He comes back a minute later wearing a wide grin. 'One drink each.'

'Sweet,' says Cam, getting up to fetch the rum from the front cabin.

I find a bottle of cola in the galley to mix with the rum and pour everyone a cup. Hunter adds the rum. Zach sniggers at Hunter's generous pours.

'What?' says Hunter. 'We're thirsty boys.'

I take a sip. The drink is so strong my eyes water.

'Hey!' Hunter says. 'We haven't started yet.'

'Okay, everyone—three fingers out,' Cam says.

I put my drink down and stick out three fingers.

'Ladies first,' Hunter says. 'Say "Never have I ever . . ." and then the thing you've never done.'

'Okay. Never have I ever played "Never have I ever".'

'That's boring!' says Hunter.

'It's smart,' says Cam, as all three of them have to put down a finger.

'Whatevs,' Hunter says. 'Never have I ever had my period.'

I roll my eyes, put a finger down, and the boys burst into laughter. The sound wakes AJ in his bunk. He rolls onto his side, props himself up on one elbow. Rubbing his eyes he asks, 'What are you playing?'

'"Never have I ever",' says Hunter.

AJ smiles. 'I love that game.'

'Join us, dude,' says Zach.

AJ wriggles out of his bunk. He's naked except for his underwear. He catches me staring.

I look down, feeling my cheeks go hot. AJ sits down beside me, his knee brushing against mine. He sticks up three fingers.

'Never have I ever had a French mum,' says Cam.

AJ puts down a finger. 'What kind of turn was that?'

'Had to even the score.'

'Okay,' Zach says. 'Never have I ever fucked a chick on a boat.'

All the boys, including Zach, put fingers down.

'You've never had sex on a boat, Oli?'

'I'm starting to believe you've never even worked on a boat,' teases Cam.

'I've never fucked a chick on a boat,' I say.

'A dude then?' says Zach.

'It's not your turn anymore.'

'Never have I ever run aground,' AJ says.

Hunter puts a finger down.

'Fucking hell,' I mutter.

Hunter shrugs. 'Wasn't my fault.'

I think of Mac telling me that when something goes wrong on a yacht, *everyone* is responsible.

'Never have I ever fallen in love with someone on a boat,' I say.

There's a long pause.

'You have to put a finger down, Oli!' says Hunter, jumping in his chair.

'What? Why?'

'Because no one has done your "Never have I ever before",' says Zach.

'Never have I ever . . .' Hunter begins. He grins. 'Never have I ever had sex with a guy on a boat.'

All eyes turn to me.

Green eyes. Blue eyes. Black eyes.

All wide open. Like a school of fish. Hanging in the water before me. Poised.

Fish eyes. Wide open. Do fish have eyelids?

'Told you,' whispers Zach.

I shiver. Thinking of the first time I had sex with Adam. How before he entered me he'd said, *You're not a virgin, are you?* How he'd managed to make virginity something to be embarrassed about.

And I could tell them that I don't mix work with play. Or simply that the opportunity has never arisen. But I feel it again now, in a flush of red, that embarrassment.

So I put down a finger.

'Ha!' screams Hunter. 'I knew it! Drink up!'

I down my drink in one go. I've lost the game either way.

There was a time when I saw something I wasn't supposed to see. Two women with red lips, all glossy and puckered. Half naked, breasts bulging. And my dad, on the sofa between them. His shirt unbuttoned, his tie on the floor, coiled like a snake. *My* dad. His hands bridging their bodies.

The look on his face. A face like sand, shifting in the wind. Unsteady. Always changing. Sand blown into shapes. The shape of desire. Of pleasure. Sand blown into surprise. Into terror. Sand blown into Rage.

It gave me power, I thought. This *seeing.* Because a mother would believe her daughter. My seeing was his undoing.

But people don't always choose to believe what they see. Or to believe what they hear. Instead, they simplify reality in order to survive it.

You don't know what you saw. Your father would never. I don't believe you. Why are you doing this to me?

The stories we tell ourselves. Bending memories. Sand blown into shapes.

Vlad sticks his head down the hatch, says to Cam, 'You and Oli are up.'

I find my wet-weather jacket and climb up the ladder into the cockpit. Cam follows me to the helm. He sits down beside me, so close our legs are touching.

Below deck, the boys are getting ready for bed. They climb into their bunks. The lights go out. And then it's just us, here, in the pink glow of the nav instruments, silent.

Cam reaches into his pocket and pulls out his phone and a set of earbuds.

'Want to listen?'

'Depends what you're listening to.'

'I've got heaps downloaded. What do you want to hear?'

'Have you heard of Unknown Mortal Orchestra?'

'I was thinking more like, um, hits . . .'

'I'll listen to whatever,' I say, picking up my earbud.

Cam puts on 'Welcome to the Jungle' by Guns N' Roses. 'I love this song.' He smiles and nudges me, his elbow prodding my bruise.

'Argh!' I cry, cupping my hand around the swelling. 'For fuck's sake.'

Thump. Tick. Thump. Tock.

'Sorry,' he says, rubbing my shoulder. 'I'll get you some more painkillers.'

'Thanks,' I mutter, and he gets up and goes down the hatch, returning minutes later with a water bottle and a handful of pills. I swallow them, pass the drink bottle back to him. He puts it in a holder beside the winch and sits back down next to me.

He wraps an arm around me gently. 'You okay?'

I nod.

'I hate seeing you like this,' he whispers.

'What?' I say, turning to face him. And then it's as if I'm seeing something I'm not supposed to see. Like I'm outside myself, wishing I wasn't seeing him lean in to kiss me.

I pull back.

A face like sand. Sand blown into shapes. The shape of desire. Into surprise.

'What?' he says. Sand blown into shame. He tries to crack a joke, but it falls dead in his lap.

'Sorry,' I say.

He removes his arm.

'I just thought . . .' he says, squirming in his seat, unable to look me in the eye.

And so I lie. 'It's just, I just don't want to while we're on the boat. You know . . . with everyone else.'

Because we don't always want to believe what we see.

Even though Cam had said, *Yeah, so fair. I feel the same*, the next day he's acting like a wounded puppy dog, tail between his legs.

When I pass him his lunch, he doesn't thank me.

When I sit beside him in the cockpit, he edges away from me.

Later, at dusk, when Vlad comes on deck with the whiteboard marker and says, 'Oli and Cam, you're on three thirty to six,' Cam snaps, 'But we've already done a darkest-hour watch.'

AJ, up on the starboard deck, jumps down into the cockpit. 'I haven't done one yet,' he says. 'Why don't I swap with Cam?'

'And go with Oli?' Vlad says.

AJ shrugs. 'Yeah, why not?'

'Sorted.' Vlad rubs out Cam's name and writes AJ's instead.

Cam looks away from me, out to the horizon. I breathe a sigh of relief.

AJ sits down opposite me in the cockpit. He smiles, and I imagine everyone else falling away until it's just he and I, here on deck. My body, tingling with excitement.

fish guts

The moon is swollen. Like my rib. Tonight, waves are swelling too. *Poseidon* lifts higher, slams down harder. My arm bangs against my bruised blue side. It's no less painful, no matter how many times.

I want to sink.

'You okay?'

'Yeah.' I wince. 'My rib's just flaring up tonight.'

'You'll be off watch soon.' AJ's smile catches in the moonlight.

I nod, as if my body hurts any less below deck.

The night is held back from black by moonlight. Beyond us is deep blue like ocean mud. Swells are outlined with silver pen. I'm cradling the bulge of my bruise now. Enduring the pain is the slightest bit easier with my right hand cupped under my left armpit. But then we hit two waves that have doubled into each other. We drop down the back of one wave and crash into the oncoming swell. Water surges across the bow and I'm washed off my seat into the cockpit, landing on my left side. I cry out. This pain has yellowed. A stab with a hot knife.

AJ helps me back to the bench seat, sits me beside him. We're both drenched and, despite the heat, I'm shivering. He wraps one arm around me.

'How are you so cold? We're in the tropics!'

We lift on another wave and I notice something beyond the bow of the boat—an enormous barrel, maybe, glowing under the moon.

'Did you see?'

We surf down into a dark trough and it disappears.

'See what?'

We rise and I point: 'There!'

AJ jumps up. 'What the hell is that?'

Suddenly a whale's tail lifts out of the sea some thirty feet away from the barrel, thirty feet closer to us than the bulk of its body.

'Holy shit!' AJ rushes to the helm. 'Hold on.'

I grip a lifeline as he throws the wheel starboard and we surf down the back of the wave at such an angle the yacht keels over. I hear plates fly out of the cupboards downstairs, smashing in the galley. I locked the cupboards. I know I locked them. There's yelling below deck.

At that moment, the tail comes down at the water with a cold, violent slap, like a hand across a face. Wet with tears. The whale raises its head to the surface and exhales through its blowhole. The clouds open up.

Fish guts rain down from the heavens.

Below deck: 'This shit fucking reeks.'

'You two aren't sleeping in the bunks, you'll stink them out,' Cam says, getting into his wet-weather gear.

AJ scoffs. 'Where else are we gonna sleep?'

'Sleep in the bow cabin.'

'There're sails in there, idiot.'

'So move them, *idiot*.'

Vlad sits up in his bunk. 'Chill, boys, alright?'

'Whatever,' AJ mutters. He grabs my hand. 'Come on, Oli.'

I follow AJ into the bow cabin. And in the moment before he shuts the door, I notice Cam glaring at me from the other side of the galley. His eyes are so sharp. They could puncture skin.

AJ moves the sails to one side of the bed, clearing enough space for one body. The boat lurches and we knock heads. His quiet laugh brushes my cheek. 'You okay?'

'Yeah.'

'Good,' he whispers, his hand sweeping my matted hair off my face, eyes smiling in the dark.

He touches my chin, gently lifting it with his thumb and forefinger. Our lips brush.

AJ is slowly. And then he's all at once.

All at once he's a tongue shoved down my throat. He's a hand reaching under my sodden top. He's a cold hand gripping the flesh of my breast like he's squeezing blood from a lemon.

And suddenly all the colours of desire, all the hands touching, and quiet words, and dimples, and eyes smiling, are extinguished like a burning wick put out with the pinch of a thumb and forefinger. AJ is a sharp pinch. Callused skin. Pinching darkness.

I push back and wedge the word, 'Wait,' in the thin corridor between his mouth and mine.

'I've been waiting to kiss you for so long.'

'AJ, stop.'

He kisses me again, pinches my nipple so hard my vision is blotted pink.

I'm choking on flesh.

'You're so fucking sexy.'

I steal a breath. The air is thick and wet.

'AJ.'

'Mm.' He grins, licks his lips. 'I love the way you say my name.'

'Please.' I can feel my throat constricting, tears welling.

Behind his shoulder, light sneaks through a tiny porthole. But down here, it isn't smooth silver. It's barbed grey.

I miss her. I miss the moon so much.

'Please . . .'

He silences me with a kiss.

Silenced with a kiss. Swept off my feet. Up against a wall. We're supposed to dream of that, aren't we?

I wriggle . . . writhe.

He thrusts his body so hard against mine I see stars and my starry-eyed kiss becomes my pants pulled to my ankles, the air as shocking as deep winter between my legs. I pull my pants up. And then I'm pulling them up again, and then again, and then again. I form a sentence with my bones; write a sentence with my body.

And then he turns the page.

I exist?

Is this what rape is? Am I about to be raped? Why aren't I fighting back? Fight back! *I am!* No you're not. Fight back. Fight back! *I can't move. I can't breathe.* Say something. *I can't breathe.*

He sticks a finger in me.

This story has so many beginnings.

There was the first time I saw AJ, when he was up the mast, looking down at me from above, whistling at me, and I was smiling inside. The time he helped me with the washing-up and our hands touched and I wanted it to last longer. The time I lied about having had sex at sea. One finger down. The time I fought with Adam in a restaurant and ended up shit-faced on an old man's boat. The time I caught my dad cheating on my mum. The first time he shut her up. There was this afternoon at dusk, when AJ switched with Cam to do the darkest-hour watch with me, and I felt really good about it. There was Cam's piercing stare and the shutting of a door. And then there was the kiss I'd wanted. A kiss I'd sought, a kiss I'd invited. Of course I did. He's great. AJ's a great guy. I like him. I liked him. The clouds open up.

Fish guts.

My spine is grinding against the hard wall of the hull. The body of the boat. Battering oncoming swells. He rips my underwear. Wedges his leg between my thighs, opening me up. Flesh cleaved apart. He undoes his fly. Bites my neck. Wriggles out of his shorts.

This is happening.

Is this really happening?

This is really happening.

And then, just like that, a thought bubbles inside me. It's a beginning; a new beginning; *my* beginning. The beginning of the story I tell myself in order to survive.

If I have sex right now, it's my decision. I'm deciding this. I'm going to have sex. I'm going to have sex with AJ. I'm deciding this right now. This is mine. I'm choosing.

I'm choosing.

We choose to breathe, don't we?

fish scales

She's an entertainer, my mum. Loves it. Loves the champagne pour and the pearls and the polished nails. Her laugh. Her painted lips. Her long, dark lashes, fluttering like black butterflies. It's all perfectly timed. Like there's a person behind her eyelids, holding up the cards. *Laugh. Smile. Blink. Blink.*

I slurped my soup. I knocked over the wine. I laughed when I was supposed to smile. Smiled when I was supposed to laugh. I was a liability.

And so she tried—my God, how she tried—to teach me. Sit up straight. Wipe your chin. *Laugh. Smile. Blink. Blink.*

She bought me the dresses, the shoes, the matching socks. She plaited my hair and tied ribbons at the end.

But then, when I was thirteen, the pimples appeared—my face was blemished. 'Must be from your father's side,' she said. 'I never had bad skin.' And everything became about the skin. The *bad* skin. And the party. *The* party of the year. At our house. And my skin. And the party. 'What will they think?'

So she took me shopping for make-up to cover and conceal. Only, my skin, my *bad* skin, didn't respond well. It was allergic to the make-up. 'Mum, it's itchy,' I said. But she wasn't listening. There were guests arriving and champagne corks popping. Pearls and polished nails.

How was the flight? Did you love New York?

By the time she turned to introduce me, my skin was raised in hives.

Laugh. Smile. Blink. Blink.

I was ushered into the bathroom, where Mae Grace helped me remove the make-up, and then sent to my room, where I stayed for the rest of the party.

Oh yes, poor Liv isn't feeling well. A cold. She must have picked it up from school.

The next day, my skin was flaking. Like fish scales drying in the sun. It was sore and red, white at the edges.

But it was nothing like *this*.

I pull down my pants, the boat lurches. I steady myself against the wall. The boat falls down the back of a swell. I fall back onto the toilet seat. Land heavy. Wince. I spread my legs, lean over. My skin is raw. It's red and sore, bruised at the edges. Flaking off. Scaly. Like fish scales drying in the sun. I start to pee and it burns. My vagina burns as if I'm lying on the deck with my legs splayed. Open to the scorching sun. Open for everyone to see. I start to cry, cupping my hand over my mouth so no one can hear me scream.

None of the boys have cleared the smashed plates from the galley.

'You *have* to lock the doors, Oli,' says Zach, standing over me as I sweep up the broken pieces. 'It's like the *first* rule,' he says.

'I did lock them,' I say. *I'm sure I did. At least, I think I did. I always lock them. Don't I? I'm sure I do.*

'Obviously not,' he mutters, putting on his board shorts.

Hunter sticks his head down the hatch. 'What's for brekkie?'

'Something we can eat with our hands,' says Zach.

'What? Why?'

'Oli didn't lock the cupboards, so all the plates smashed when we almost hit that whale. I don't know how you slept through it.'

Hunter shakes his head. 'That's like rule number one when you work a galley, Oli.'

'So I've heard,' I say, picking up the final pieces. 'I'll make sandwiches.'

Up on deck, I hand out sandwiches to Hunter and Zach. Vlad and Cam are below deck, asleep. AJ comes into the cockpit with a jerry can, dripping oil on the deck.

He holds it up. 'This is leaking.'

'Chuck it,' says Hunter.

AJ shrugs, then lobs it over the side. It lands with a splash, then begins to sink, oil slick swirling like words uttered in another time.

He leans over the side, washes the mess off his hands, then takes a seat in the cockpit. When I pass him his sandwich, he winks at me. I imagine it like a lizard's slimy third eyelid, sliding horizontally. My spine curls.

'I saw that,' remarks Hunter. 'This flirting is making me sick.'

'No on-board romance, please,' says Zach.

AJ laughs. The sound is sour green. Under my skin. In me.

'Too late, I think!' Hunter says, pointing at my neck.

'For fuck's sake,' Zach mutters.

'AJ and Oli sitting in a tree,' sings Hunter, 'K-I-S-S-I-N-G.'

AJ flicks Hunter's ear. 'Grow up,' he says, and Hunter giggles.

I walk across the cockpit to sit at the helm with Zach. As I pass AJ, I feel him tap me on the bum. My whole body shudders. It makes Hunter's laugh thicken.

'I think we should try to catch a fish today,' I say, desperate to change the subject.

'Great idea, Oli,' says Zach, getting up to fetch two fishing reels from under his seat. 'Should we make it a competition?'

'AJ's already caught his,' Hunter manages, then cracks up again.

This time AJ laughs too.

'Yeah, yeah,' says Zach dryly. 'Very funny.' He attaches the reels to the boat, one on the port rail and one on the starboard. 'Oli and I are blue reel. You idiots are red. Loser has to gut it.'

'What kind of bet is that?' AJ smirks. 'I'd happily gut it.'

Hunter laughs. 'Mate, you're fucked.'

'Do you know the best way to kill a fish?' asks Zach.

'Pour alcohol into its gills,' I say.

'How'd you know that?'

'A friend told me.'

He nods and sits back down beside me. 'I underestimated you,' he says, quietly so that the other two don't hear.

I open my mouth to speak, to tell him, *Yeah, you did . . .* But before my words fully form, the fishing line behind Zach tweaks, slackens, and then pulls tight. He jumps up, shouts, 'We got one!'

Hunter says, 'I'll get the rum,' and disappears downstairs. By the time he's back on deck, Zach is landing the fish in the cockpit. Hunter unscrews the bottle.

'We're not wasting the rum,' AJ says, pushing Hunter out of the way. He reaches down and unlatches the winch handle from the winch. 'Give it here,' he says to Zach, who kicks the fish across the cockpit.

Watching the fish flounder, I think how instant this death could be, with Hunter's rum. Straight into the gills. How nice. Because three minutes is an awfully long time when you can't breathe.

You don't even know how long that is. It's disgustingly long. Because it's not just the sex, how dry and how suffocating it is, the occupation of space, the invasion of your home. The pollution. How they make your skin stretch for their body, how they make you tear.

It's all the other ways they make you stretch too, make you stretch into hours as you lie awake with their breath scraping against your neck, like a knife scraping fish scales off your slimy body. Lying awake, just waiting for the sun to rise, lying there with cum oozing out of you, waiting for the moon to disappear because you can't bear for her to see you like this.

It would be so much kinder to pour alcohol into your gills, straight into your brain.

But he doesn't. AJ doesn't want to waste the rum, so he bludgeons the fish with the winch handle. Again. And again. Because the damn thing won't stop squirming. And, even when the fish goes limp, its face now mutilated, head caved in, I'm not convinced that it won't feel the hook pulled out of its lips, that it won't feel the red sting of each individual scale being scraped off. Scales like shards of glass floating in a pool of blood, glinting in the sun.

Below deck, Cam is climbing out of his bunk. He rubs his eyes, looks at me, his vision focusing. 'What the fuck is that on your neck?'

I feel my neck, feel the bruise. Feel the *love* bite at the hollow of my throat.

'It was AJ, wasn't it?'

I nod.

'Did you have sex with him?'

'He had sex with me.'

Or maybe I should say: He had sex on me, in me. He stuck his dick in something. He put something in me. Had to force it because it wouldn't go in. That happens, you know. Clamshell closes, pink lips sealing to protect black pearl. Closing, shutting, squeezing, sealing, shutting up, I shut up. And then I moaned, because I chose to have sex. I'm choosing to have sex. This is the sound you're meant to make when you're choosing to have sex. This is the sound you make when it feels good, wow, so good my leg is shaking. My body is shaking. I moan. It's the sound you make when someone is having sex *at* you, so deep I have my palm on my belly and I can feel him thrusting, feel him pushing from the inside out. And my leg, it's shaking because he's so deep. I'm deep blue ocean mud. So deep in ocean my eardrums burst. And my body is shaking because I think maybe he'll thrust out through my belly button so I push back down on my belly with my hand, trying to hold my flesh together.

'Are you fucking serious?' Cam says. He is furious.

I exhale in relief . . . my body is heard. I'm heard. He hears me.

'Yes.'

Cam shakes his head, says, 'I can't believe you'd do this to me.'

'Wait, *what*?'

'I *liked* you!' he says, spitting his words at me. 'And now I have to look at him every day. I mean, couldn't you have at least waited till you were off the boat?'

'*He* had sex with me.'

'So what? You didn't want it?'

I don't say anything. Silence pools.

'Is that what you're trying to say?'

The sound of no sound is sick yellow.

'That he raped you?'

'I'm not going to say that.'

'So he didn't rape you?'

'It's not like that,' I say, holding onto my belly, something pushing from the inside out. 'It's . . . it's complicated.'

There was black and white, like when I pulled my pants up for the fourth time and said, *No.* And then there was grey, like when I took my top off, like when I bent over and stuck my arse out. Like when I took him in my mouth, because that hurt less. Black and white, like when he pushed so hard on the back of my head I gagged and threw up into my mouth.

'There's an in between.'

Cam says, 'He either raped you or he didn't.'

I'm whispering. But I want to scream. 'We're in the middle of the fucking ocean, Cam! I'm not using that word.'

Rape.

Rape is the deepest red I've ever seen.

'Oli, if he raped you, I'll kill him.'

'That's why! If I use that word, the shit will hit the fan.'

'But if he did it, he should be punished.'

I can feel AJ in me.

'I don't want any of this,' I say, tears welling.

'Well, why did you tell me then?'

Holding onto my belly, I say, 'You asked.' I sit back onto a bunk and my body folds over, folds in two.

'I don't even know if I believe you.'

'What?'

I can feel AJ. He's in me. He's in me! I can't breathe. He's in me. Like sour blood, like curdled milk. My bruised rib is pulsing. I can smell his cum on me, sticky on flaky skin, fish scales scraped away. Slice fish open, guts spew out. Slice my belly. Watch him spew out. Fish guts. This shit reeks.

'Like, I don't know whether to feel sorry for you, or hate you.'

'You should believe me.'

Cam looks me square in the face. Those piercing eyes; they could puncture skin. What happens when you puncture an eyeball, when you stick a pin in it? Does it burst? What gushes out? I imagine my eyeball like a water balloon, full of mucus and sick yellow fluid, sick yellow like my silence, the sound of no sound. Stick a pin in my eye and my eyeball bursts, sick raining down my cheeks like fish guts from the heavens.

He shakes his head. 'I don't think I do . . . If mean, if you didn't want it, why didn't you just scream?'

fish blood

There are stretch marks on the sea.

Why didn't I *just* scream?

I roll over in my bunk.

Again and again.

I roll over in my bunk.

Why didn't I just scream? It's a ringing in my ears.

Again and again. Like pulling my pants up. Again and again.

It's fucking relentless.

Why didn't I *just* scream?

As if someone would have heard me scream when he was *just* inches away and couldn't hear *no*.

As if that's all it would have taken.

A scream.

As if that would have saved me.

I roll over in my bunk.

And feel a wetness. A wetness between my thighs.

'Oh, shit,' I whisper, sitting up, parting my legs. My undies are soaked. It's all over the bunk.

I blink and tears slip down my cheeks.

I climb out of my bunk and hurry through the cabin into the bathroom. Grabbing handfuls of toilet paper, I pull off my pants and wipe myself clean, throwing the bloodied paper in the toilet.

A moment later, it hits me what I've done. 'Oh my God,' I mutter, 'you *idiot*.' I try to fish out the paper from the bowl. But it's already started to break apart. I get out the biggest clumps and put them in the plastic bag we're using for a bin. I hope I'll get lucky and be able to flush the rest away.

I shift the lever to the right and fill the bowl with fresh sea water. Then I shift the lever again and begin to pump. At first, it's fine. And then it's not. '*Fuck*.' I can feel the wetness between my thighs, can feel it trickling down my leg. The boat lurches and the bathroom door swings open. I almost fall out of the bathroom, grabbing the sink to save myself. The door swings shut with a sudden bang. It surges through me.

I grab more paper and wipe my leg. I stuff a handful between my legs and squeeze them together to hold it there. I try pumping the flush again, but it's no use. I've clogged the toilet.

I shut the lid and go to my rucksack stored behind the nav station. Riffling through its contents, I find four loose tampons. My period is early. Too early. I'm not prepared. It never comes early. Tears are streaming now as I shuffle back to the bathroom, put the paper in the bin, and insert a tampon.

I feel it go in. Slowly. Feel all of it. The dryness of it. Coarse and ribbed. My body seizing up. Clam shell closing. So that I have to shove hard to get it into myself.

I throw my bloodied undies in the bin in the galley and start making breakfast. I boil the last of the eggs. Then it's on to the non-perishables. Packets of cereal with mini cartons of long-life milk. Now that we don't have any bowls to eat from, I pour the milk into the plastic packets within the cereal boxes and pass them around with spoons.

'Aren't you gonna eat, Oli?' asks Zach.

Beneath the brooding sky, I lie and tell him I've already eaten.

My insides growl. I press my palm against my stomach, pushing down hard. Silencing my body. Because feeling empty feels better than being occupied.

After they've finished, Hunter, who took the last watch, goes below deck to sleep.

'What the fuck!' he shouts from the cabin.

The other boys rush through the cockpit and huddle around the hatch. 'What is it?' asks Vlad.

'There's black stuff all through my bunk!'

Vlad disappears down the hatch, the others following.

'That's blood!' says Vlad.

I hear Zach ask, 'Who slept in this bunk?'

'Oli did,' says AJ.

I hold my breath.

'Oh my God,' says Zach finally. 'I think it's period blood.'

Hunter screams, 'Yuck!'

I tuck my knees up and hold myself in a ball. As small as I can. Squeeze tight. Hold still.

Then there's more commotion up the front of the cabin. Muffled voices below deck. Someone's found the toilet, clogged. A bowl of blood and seawater.

Vlad comes up on deck, his face hot red. He's fuming. 'What the hell have you done to the toilet?' he says. 'Everyone's got to use that.'

'I know, I'm sorry. I wasn't thinking,' I say, welling up again. 'I tried to clear it.'

'Well, it didn't work,' he says, then mutters to himself, 'I knew you were a bad idea.'

The other boys all come up the hatch into the cockpit. They stand over me, sea vultures circling.

'Yeah,' Cam says, 'it's completely fucked.'

Tears slide free, one after the other, like rain.

'Where are we going to shit?' Hunter asks.

'Yeah, I need to go now,' says Zach.

'Over the side, I guess,' Vlad says, huffing.

'I'm sorry!'

Cam glares at me. 'Yeah. You should be.'

I get up. 'I'll try and fix it.'

'Gross!' shrieks Hunter.

I turn around to see a smudge of red on the seat where I've been sitting.

'It stinks,' says Cam.

'Fuck off,' I say. 'No it doesn't.'

'Smells like fish blood!' Hunter says.

AJ looks at me. 'What are we going to do with you?'

'Stick her in the dinghy,' Hunter says, and both he and AJ burst into laughter.

'That's the first good idea you've had all trip,' says Cam, laughing too now.

'You can't be serious,' I say.

'Yeah, come on,' says Zach. 'Stop kidding around.'

Cam's smile disappears. 'I'm not.'

Hunter's laughter fades. 'Cam, wait,' he says. 'I was only joking.'

'I'm dead serious.'

I look him in the eye. 'You are a cunt.'

'What did you say to me?' he demands, his face twisting, contorting. Twitching with rage. He grabs my shoulder, scoops me up under the thighs, lifting me into the air.

I scream. 'Put me down!'

Cam pinches my thighs. Yells something at Hunter, ordering him to draw in the dinghy.

'Stop it!' shouts Zach. 'Put her down!'

Cam ignores him.

I whip my head around to see Hunter standing at the stern. Frozen like a stunned fish.

'Do it, Hunter!' bellows Cam.

I see the words jolt Hunter, like a shock of electricity.

'*Now!*'

Reluctantly, Hunter starts pulling the dinghy in towards the back of the boat.

'Put me down!' I shout, punching Cam in the back with my fists. I'm writhing and wriggling. Scratching and clawing. He tightens his grip, edges towards the back of the boat.

'Cut it out!' Zach yells at him. 'You can't do this!'

I look over Cam's shoulder to see AJ shove Zach. Hard. He falls back onto the deck.

I catch Zach's gaze. Pleading with him. *Help.*

But he retreats into the cockpit.

'Cam, please,' I say, starting to sob. 'Please!'

He digs his fingers into my flesh. 'Shut up,' he says. 'You stupid slut.'

Hunter has the dinghy at the back of the boat now.

Cam looks back at Vlad, who's still standing in the cockpit, watching on impassively. *'Vlad!'* I scream. *'VLAD!'*

He looks from me to Cam, saying nothing. Sick yellow silence floods the cockpit.

'Fucking arsehole!' I shout and his eyes widen, the blow of my insult reverberating through him. He flinches. Then he turns away.

And that's all the encouragement Cam needs.

He drops me a metre down into the dinghy.

I land on my side in a flash of purple. My vision blurs as they let out the rope and I drift further away, until I'm several metres behind the boat, being dragged along like a fish hooked on the end of a line.

The clouds open up in the late afternoon.

Up ahead, Hunter is hanging over the back of the boat, doing a shit. It hits the water, bobs past the dinghy. There's laughter in the cockpit.

My throat is parched now. Sunlight beating down, drawing the moisture out of me. Like bleached coral. I grab hold of the rope and start pulling myself in towards the boat. Hunter sees and points to me, muttering something to the others.

Cam, near the back of the cockpit, grabs the fish knife and kneels down, threatening to cut the rope, a grin twisting across his face.

I let go. The slackened rope sinks, then pulls tight.

I turn away from them. Searching the monochrome for detail. The ocean like a painting. A site for yearning.

I think of her body. Memories and desires. Robynne. Dissolving like ice into the grey. And I see, now. How easily I could just slip away. We choose. Don't we?

The wind has picked up now, blowing from behind us. The boys have the boom out wide and a pole propping out the headsail. Vlad is at the helm, steering starboard, then edging port to lessen the rolls of the boat as it sails downwind.

I sit back in the dinghy. Despite the heat, I'm shivering. There's blood leaking from me, dark red on the white seat. I wrap my arms around myself. Holding myself together. Like if I let go, my body might break apart like skin underwater.

Ahead, I see Vlad leave the cockpit to go down the hatch. Hunter takes over at the helm. He's not nearly as experienced as Vlad, and the boat begins to roll heavily. Soon the end of the boom starts dipping into the water.

I watch it rolling back and forth, back and forth, dipping deeper into the sea with each roll.

Too deep. The sails slacken. A gust moves past me. It stretches across the ocean between the dinghy and the yacht, like rippled darkness. Reaches the stern. Rises up. Fills the sails. Full. And then something snaps.

The boom breaks in a burst of blue, the bang ricocheting out across the water, into nothing. Into no one.

There's shouting on board. Screaming.

Vlad comes bounding up into the cockpit, followed by AJ. They're all in the cockpit now, scampering like rats.

'*Holy shit*,' I mutter, eyeing the broken boom.

I start pulling myself in, against the wake, against the tide. Rope burn sets my palms on fire, but I keep pulling, one hand after the other, my torso cramping, until I'm at the stern of the boat, reaching up to grab the lifeline.

I grip the yacht with one hand, use the other to steady myself, then grab hold of the ladder and haul myself up into the cockpit.

Zach and AJ are dropping the sails. Cam is at the helm, trying desperately to steady the boat. Vlad screams at Hunter. It's a wash of yellow. Sick and panicked.

I climb up onto the port deck to inspect the damage.

'Get down from there!' Vlad yells at me.

'The preventer was tied to the vang!' I shout.

AJ jumps down into the cockpit. 'Yeah—where it's supposed to be!'

'No!' I shout. 'You have to tie it to the *end* of the boom. Otherwise *this* happens. It breaks!'

'How would you know?' snaps Hunter.

The question courses through me. And then all the others. In waves. *Are you sure, Oli? Have you worked on a boat before, Oli? Don't you know to close the cupboard, Oli? Did he rape you or not, Oli? Why didn't you just scream?*

'Because I'm not a fucking idiot!' I shout. And then I'm shouting all kinds of things. Until it all blurs together.

'Shut up!' Vlad bellows. 'Shut. The. Fuck. Up!'

'Fuck you, Vlad!' I scream. 'This is *your* fault.'

'I can't take this,' he says, throwing his hands up in the air. Shoving Hunter out of the way, he reaches up and grabs me by the wrist, yanks me down into the cockpit. He pulls me towards the hatch, fingers digging into my flesh. He jerks me forwards, down the ladder, below deck, pulling me through the belly of the boat to the front cabin. There, he picks me up and throws me. I land between sail bags and a fishing rod. Winded. Gasping for breath.

I scramble to my feet as the door closes with a slam. I try to open it, but he's pushing against it from the other side. His weight, against mine.

I shout, 'Let me out! You can't do this! Vlad! Please! Let me out! Open the door! Please. Please.' I whimper. '*Please.*' But it's his word against mine.

fish bladder

Night falls in the cabin. *Falls.* Like falling water.

All around me are sail bags, like bags of skin. I curl into a ball and think of something someone said to me once. In another time. On another sea. In the blink of an eye. Something about how you don't really notice the darkness, not until you're right in the thick of it. Not until the streetlights come on and you look around and think, *Shit, it just got dark quick.*

Just like that. Darkness is total. So black I can't tell if my eyes are open or shut. The moon blacked out. The stars a million miles away. So dark. That if it weren't for the steady rumble of the motor, I'd believe I were dead.

In this pocket of darkness, I can't see that the cabin is barely wider than my arms or that there's fishing gear piled against the wall. I can't see the folds in the sails. Or AJ's cum stain on the mattress. In this pocket of darkness. I'm as safe as dead.

Caught in the in-between, I imagine the earth is rocking. It's all back and forth, back and forth.

But now I'm coming to, and there's drool caked to my chin and fur on my teeth, and I'm peeling apart puffy eyelids to see the sun through a skylight that's only a few feet above my head. The sun is swinging back and forth in the sky and I realise the earth really is rocking. I prop myself up on one elbow. My head is pounding like someone's clobbered me with a brick. I look around and, as the room comes into focus, I wait for this all to make sense. But it doesn't. The walls are curved, and no wider than the bed—if you'd even call this a bed. I'm lying on a wafer-thin mattress, wedged between a huge canvas bag and a fishing rod. There's a weird thumping outside and, when I look up, the sun is still swinging. I feel a tightening in my chest, a fierce contraction of my ribcage, like my breath is caught and can't get out. Where the fuck *am* I?

I could be anywhere. Any time. Any sea.

But then I feel the wetness. And when I look down at the red mess between my legs, it all falls into place, all the pieces lining up in rows like fish scales.

There are no roses here. I'm on *Poseidon*.

There's a pain in my abdomen. I need to pee. I climb out of the bed. I can hear voices below deck. Cam and AJ. I pound the door with my fists. The voices quieten.

I stop hitting the door. Pause a moment. Listen.

'Just ignore her.'

'She's fucking crazy.'

I scream.

And then I collapse back into myself. Fish bladder emptying, soaking the mattress.

Maggie, I wish you'd told me. At sea, no one can hear you scream.

medusa

Milky black eyes. Medusa. I bite. Sinking fangs. Into his arm. Flesh swelling purple veins. Bursting. With hot green venom. Like snake eyes turning men to stone. Statues. Lined up below deck.

The boat lurches. I wake in a burst.

There are footsteps behind the door. The door is wrenched open. A gust of fresh air comes over me in a wave. I breathe in deep.

Vlad looks me up and down, disgust on his face.

'We'll be in Auckland Harbour in the next hour,' he mutters, then leaves me. Medusa. Covered in blood and piss.

Everyone is upstairs in the cockpit when I crawl out of the bow cabin into the main body of the boat. I find a tampon in my bag and fresh clothes, and change behind the nav station, afraid that if I go back into the bow, the door might swing shut behind me, locking me in. Forever.

When I come on deck, back into the light of day, I'm silent.

So silent, even my breath passes without sound.

Above me, the broken boom is tied down. Vlad is at the helm, motoring us in.

When we dock in Auckland, Hunter says to Cam, 'You excited to see Amy?'

Cam shrugs. 'A newborn kinda kills the romance.'

'Who's Amy?' asks Zach.

'His fiancée,' Hunter answers.

Cam looks to me. I shudder.

'Do you have a phone?' I ask the barmaid in the yacht club.

'Sorry, love. What did you say?'

'Do you have a phone?'

She shakes her head.

I feel tears welling, my eyes glazing over.

'You can use my mobile, if you like?'

I nod. I dial, bring the phone to my ear. It rings out.

I try again.

Maggie picks up on the fourth ring.

'Hello?'

I try to speak, but nothing comes out.

'Hello?' she repeats.

I begin to sob.

'Oli?' she says, suddenly worried. 'Oli, is that you?'

I take a deep breath. 'Get me out of here.'

desert

pale blue sand

I hate this. This looking without seeing. I scan the bar, and then the couches. Walk through one room into another. Out into the beer garden. Half smiling at faces I don't know. Hoping one will smile back. Hoping one, the right one, will light up and open and unfold.

Why did I let Natasha talk me into this?

The beer garden of the Faltering Fullback is tiered, layer upon layer of plants and wood. Pint glasses and twists of smoke.

Why had she suggested *this* pub for a blind date?

I spy a guy sitting alone with a full pint of beer. I hint at a smile. He grins.

Edging closer, I say, 'Hugo?'

'I could be.'

'What?'

'Sit down and I'll be anyone you want me to be.'

I roll my eyes, turn and push through the door back into the pub. The room is heaving. A guy steps backwards onto my foot.

'Sorry,' he mutters.

'No worries,' I say, pushing past him. *This was a bad idea*, I think, rounding the bar, making for the front door.

And then I see him from the corner of my eye. A man looking just as lost as me, his eyes darting around the room. Looking without seeing. He's wearing jeans and a t-shirt. A green fleece, unzipped. Thin brown hair, round glasses and two sleeper earrings in his left ear.

He hasn't seen me yet. I could still leave. But there's something that keeps me here. Something in the way he holds himself. Tall and lean, though he's slouching a little. Like he's spent his life trying to appear shorter. It's endearing, this modesty.

I catch his eye. His face lights up, opens, unfolds. And as he breathes a sigh of relief, I feel him come over me in a wave. A warm wash of excitement and awe. The way I once felt entering the ocean, diving down, the water combing through my hair, sweeping it back off my shoulders, so that everything untangles and spreads out wide.

He moves through the crowd, eyes locked on mine. Reaching me, he offers his hand. I take it. We shake.

'At last,' he says.

I smile. 'At last.'

We take our wines out into the beer garden, finding a table between palm fronds and knots of ivy. In the cold, we exhale in tiny clouds when we speak.

'So how long have you worked for Natasha?' he asks.

'Almost two years now.'

'Wow,' he says.

I laugh. 'Your sister is not easy to work for.'

'So I've heard.'

'But it's worth it,' I say. 'She's fierce . . . and fearless. It's very inspiring.'

He smiles. 'I bet.'

I take a sip of wine.

'What about before?'

'Pardon me?'

'I mean, before Natasha, where were you working?'

'In a small commercial gallery in Greenwich.'

'Which one?'

'Willow Gallery.'

'I know the one,' he says. 'Very impressive.'

I shrug. 'I got lucky.'

'What do you mean?'

'A friend of mine opened the gallery with Lindy in the late eighties.'

'Lindy Harrs,' he says. 'Another fierce woman.'

'She certainly is. I actually lived with her when I first arrived in London.'

'You did get lucky,' he says with a gentle smile. 'So who's the friend that introduced you to Lindy?'

'Oh,' I say. 'Margaret Walker.'

'Maggie? You know she mentored my sister, right?'

'Yeah,' I say, 'I know. Natasha came to the first show I helped curate at Willow and we got talking, worked out we both knew Maggie . . . I think her assistant had just moved to New York or something. Anyway, a week later she offered me the job.'

'Well, I'm glad she did.'

'Why?'

'Because I might not have met you otherwise.'

I feel my cheeks warm. I look away from him.

'You know this was my idea?' he says.

'What? The blind date?'

He nods, smiling sheepishly. 'We sort of met last year, actually.'

'Ha! Really?' I ask, immediately regretting my obvious surprise.

'At an opening at Tash's gallery,' he says, playing with a beer coaster. 'I was home for the holidays.'

'Which show?'

'Kate Ballis.'

'I was there. Of course. I don't think we were introduced though . . . were we?'

He shakes his head. 'No. But I saw you.' He puts down the coaster, looks up, looks into me. 'I saw you, and I wanted to meet you.'

And there's something in the curve of his smile, in the soft slouch of his shoulders, in the warm edge of this moment, that makes time pass effortlessly. Like I don't have to hold my own. I don't have to hold anything. Because he's opened a space for me to relax into.

When I come back from the bathroom, there are two new glasses of wine waiting with Hugo at the table.

'You bought the last round!' I say.

He shrugs. 'I don't mind.'

'Are you trying to get me drunk?'

His eyes widen. 'What? No!'

I take a seat. 'I'm kidding. Sorry. Terrible joke.'

'Yeah, not the finest material,' he says, laughing.

'Tell me about you,' I say, eager to change the subject. 'What's your story?'

'My story? Ha! Well, I don't want to bore you . . .'

'You won't.'

'What do you want to know?'

'Natasha said you've just come back from the States. What were you doing there?'

'My PhD,' he says, 'at Berkeley.'

'PhD in what?'

'Environmental sciences,' he says. 'I was looking at the way deserts are transforming as a result of climate change.'

'And what did you find?'

'That it's hard to feel good about humankind.'

I sit back in my chair. 'What do you mean?'

'Some of us can be incredibly destructive. And what's worse is that the people in power don't seem to care.'

'Some of them care.'

'Not enough,' he says.

I take another sip of wine.

'That's why your work is so important,' he tells me.

'*My* work?' I say. 'I work in a swanky art gallery. How's that important?'

'Art moves people, Oli. I find the facts, but *art* communicates it in a way that engages people. After all, if we were purely rational beings, we wouldn't be in this mess.'

I shrug. 'I'm not an artist.'

'Yeah, but you're the one who decides whose work is seen—that's power.'

I finish my wine, look over to Hugo to see if he wants another, but he's barely touched his. 'You don't like the wine?' I ask.

He smiles. Shrugs. 'Just trying to make this last as long as I can.'

As if on cue, a security guard approaches the table.

'Sorry, folks. Time to go.'

I check my watch. 'Wow,' I say, grinning at Hugo. 'Time flies when you're having fun.'

He stands up, leaving his nearly full glass of wine on the table and we reach for our scarves.

As I loop my scarf around my neck, one of my dangly earrings gets caught. Hugo helps me to unhook it.

'Thanks,' I say.

He holds the earring up, studying it. 'I like these,' he says.

'I like yours,' I reply.

'Let's swap—one of my hoops for one of your dangly ones.' He grins. 'That way you'll have to see me again.'

I can feel myself blushing. 'I'd like that,' I say. He undoes one of the sleepers and passes it to me, then puts my earring in its place. He shakes his head theatrically so that the earring swishes back and forth, silver glinting beneath a garden light.

Then he takes my hand, and we walk out of the pub together. And I smile, because when our skin meets it feels like we've been here before. Like rain returning to a desert, a landscape remembering. Pale blue sand.

Wildflowers blooming. If only for a day.

pink sand

I arrive first and unlock the gallery. It's all white walls and polished concrete. We're showing photographer Tom Blachford. Palm Springs lit by moonlight. I stop by my favourite, sipping my morning coffee. Long exposures leave the sky dusty blue. I feel myself drawn into it. Like I'm sleepwalking between iridescent fronds and glowing pools. Mountains half awake, caught in a distant dream. Moonlight flooding the landscape. A seabed of houses. Silver, with angular roofs. And windows, opening into the unknown.

I take a seat at my desk, scrolling through emails with one hand, the other playing with the sleeper in my ear. Thinking of the walk to Finsbury Park station. How I'd wanted the walk to stretch on. Thinking of the almost-kiss. The awkwardness of it. The sweetness of it.

Natasha comes into the gallery in a burst of talk. At first I think she's addressing me, then I realise she's on her earpiece.

She talks louder than anyone I know, as if the distance between her and the person on the other end of the line warrants raising her voice ten notches.

She's wearing her trademark black suit, eyeliner and bold red lipstick, her cropped hair riding at a sharp angle across her cheek.

'Okay, excellent,' she says. 'See you very soon . . . Bye now.' Strutting over to me, she takes out the earpiece and picks up the coffee that is waiting for her on my desk.

'Morning,' I say.

'How was it?' she asks immediately.

'No way,' I say.

'Oh, come on!'

'You're my boss. This is weird!'

'I'm your friend,' she says.

'He's your brother!'

'Yeah. But you can at least tell me the vibe.'

'It was nice. He's really nice.'

'Will you see him again?'

I nod.

'Good. That's what he said.'

'So you've spoken to him?'

'Of course I have.'

'What did he say?'

'Oh, so *now* you want to talk about it?'

I roll my eyes.

She laughs, then tells me, 'Cloudy Robertson just landed. She's all locked in for dinner tomorrow night.'

'When's her work arriving?'

'Why are you asking me? This is *your* show.'

'Sorry,' I say, 'just thinking aloud.'

'I need you to be on top of this.'

'I am,' I tell her.

'Good,' she says, taking a sip of coffee. 'Nail it and this show will be huge.'

I sit back in my chair and think of Maggie. Of her first all-woman show. *What was important was that* I *saw those women. And they saw each other . . . Because even as women, we don't always see each other.*

I pick up one of the publicity brochures for *WOMXN,* my first all-woman show, and put it in my bag, thinking, *I must send this to Maggie.*

After lunch, I'm standing in front of one of Blachford's photos, speaking about the work to two prospective buyers, when I see Hugo wander into the gallery. I immediately lose my train of thought. 'Sorry, I . . .'

Natasha jumps in. 'I'll take it from here,' she says, then whispers, 'You have a visitor.'

I excuse myself from the group and walk over to meet Hugo.

'Sorry to ambush you at work,' he says, his cheeks reddening. 'I have the afternoon off and was hoping you might be able to join me for a walk.'

Natasha calls across the gallery, 'Of course she can.'

'I guess I'm free then,' I say. 'Let me just grab my coat.'

We walk along the Thames beneath an ashen sky. The river is a washed-out brown. Windblown, like a creased cloth. It's late autumn and the festive season is drawing near; coloured lights are strung up in laneways and South Bank is lined with Christmas trees.

'My birthday is in December,' Hugo says. 'When I was a kid, I used to think the decorations were for my birthday.'

'How old are you turning?'

'Twenty-nine.'

'Oh! We're almost the same age,' I say. 'I turn twenty-nine in March.'

He smiles and takes my hand. 'Wow!' he exclaims. 'Your hand is freezing.' Hugo rubs it between both of his.

'I'm cold-blooded,' I say and Hugo laughs.

I look up and see the London Eye. 'Can you believe I've lived here for three years and still haven't been on that thing?'

'Can you believe I was born and raised in London and I haven't been on it either?'

I say, 'We'll have to then.'

'Oh, um . . .' He sounds hesitant.

'Come on!' I say. 'I've always wanted to go on it.'

'But—'

'It'll be great,' I assure him, leading him towards the giant Ferris wheel, with its long white arms and glass eyes.

We line up behind a group of schoolchildren. There's screaming and giggling and hitting. One kid turns around and eyes us suspiciously. 'You're really tall,' she says.

'Thank you,' I say, teasing.

'Not you!' the girl squeals. *'Him!'*

Another girl turns around. 'Is he your husband?'

'I'm her cat,' says Hugo.

'You're not a cat! You're a man!'

'Meow!' Hugo says, and the little girls crack up laughing.

'Come on now,' their teacher says, ushering them onto the Ferris wheel.

'Are you coming with us?' one of the girls calls out.

I shake my head. 'We'll take the next one. There's not enough room for me and my cat.'

'Bye, cat lady!' the girls squeal.

'Goodbye!'

'Meow, meow,' Hugo says, waving.

The door of the capsule closes on their giggles and the kids set off. The next pod comes along and we step inside. Hugo takes a deep breath. When he exhales, his breath quivers.

'Are you okay?' I ask, suddenly noticing how pale he is, as if all the colour has drained from his face.

He nods, pursing his lips.

'Are you sure?'

The door closes and he squeezes my hand. The capsule starts to move. His legs quake. 'Oh God,' he whispers.

'Seriously, are you okay?'

'Can we sit down?'

'What?' I ask, but Hugo's legs are already giving out. He falls down in a heap. Hyperventilating now.

'Oh shit,' I mutter, understanding, now, his hesitancy.

All around us, people are staring. But as we lift higher from the ground, the sky seems to close in, like everything is becoming smaller, clouds wrapping around us, until it's only him and I, here in the iris. I sit down in front of him, take both of his hands. His eyes are shut. 'Open your eyes,' I whisper.

He opens one eye, then the other, his gaze darting around the capsule.

'Just look at me,' I say, smiling, and his gaze settles on mine. 'Just us.'

Hugo squeezes my hands again.

'Breathe,' I whisper. 'Ready? In.'

We inhale together.

'And out.'

We exhale together.

'In . . . and out.'

He leans in closer. I lean in closer. Until our foreheads are pressed together. And we're closing our eyes. Noses gently brushing. Lips touching. Like land coming into focus.

When we step out of the capsule, Hugo's legs are still shaking.

'Why did you suggest going on the London Eye if you're scared of heights?' I ask.

'I didn't,' he says.

'Yes, you did.'

'I just asked if you'd been on it,' he protests, and I laugh.

'Whoops.'

'I'm sorry you didn't get to see the view,' he says.

'Don't worry,' I say. 'We'll just have to go again . . .'

He chuckles. 'I like your optimism.'

'Where to now then?'

Hugo smiles. 'The Tate?'

'I'll show you my favourite painting,' I say. 'Don't worry. It's on the ground floor.'

And so we wander through the Tate, weaving between Rothko reds and Dali pinks, all the way through to Yves Klein's *IKB 79*.

'So this is your favourite?'

I nod, a grin widening.

'Why?'

'Because no matter how close up and palpable the canvas is, the blue is always about distance . . . Something absent.'

He takes hold of my hand, interlacing his fingers with mine, and looks into the painting. Into the blue. Into everything and nothing.

'What's your favourite?' I whisper.

'I'll show you,' he says, leading me back through the gallery to a portrait of a man holding a young girl in a blackened rock pool. 'This one.'

'Why?'

'My answer is not as clever as yours,' he says.

'Try me.'

'Because it's a beautiful moment. But something about it feels haunted.'

I look into the painting. Into the water. Smooth and dark. Bodies unnaturally lit in the night. Teal rocks and pink flesh.

'I like that the painting can be two things at once,' he says.

When we come out of the Tate, night is all around us. 'I forgot about these early sunsets,' he says, 'living in California for so long. I got used to the daylight. Forgot how much I hate it getting dark at three in the afternoon.'

'The dark is my favourite thing about London,' I say.

'Really?' He sounds disbelieving.

'Yeah. It's intimate. I like the way it seems to close down around me. Everything feels closer.'

He shakes his head. 'I love the summer. The days stretching long into the night . . .'

And I want to say that I don't like the openness of summer in London, the openness of the light. How it makes me feel exposed. Like spread legs.

But I don't. Because dating is in the realm of nice stories.

Cloudy Robertson arrives at the gallery and she is every bit as wild as her work. With piercing blue eyes, a hard brow, striking cheekbones and a shock of pink hair.

Her paintings had arrived not long before she did. Mountain ranges with dark skies and acidic green seas are stacked at the back of the gallery, along with Vivienne's portraits, Holly's sandstone sculptures and the projector for Mikaela's light installation.

'Blachford?' says Cloudy, eyeing the last photo to come down off the wall.

'Yes,' Natasha says. 'He sold out.'

'And so will you,' I say, walking over to greet her. 'Your work is even more incredible in the flesh.'

'Thank you,' she says.

I extend my hand. 'I'm Oli.'

'Cloudy.'

'So nice to finally meet you.'

'And you,' she says.

'This is Natasha,' I say, and they shake hands as well.

'Shall we go for a drink?' Natasha suggests.

The two of us agree and I fetch our coats. Natasha's is an extravagant black fur coat, which she promises is fake. Mine is a denim jacket with a black hood sewn into it. Cloudy, like her paintings, is wearing as many colours as you could possibly fit into one outfit.

Outside, the evening air nips at our heels. 'Fuck me, it's freezing!' Cloudy exclaims.

'Welcome to England,' I say.

'I was at the beach in Sydney this time last week,' she says. 'Forty-two degrees!'

'You're kidding.'

'Summer hasn't even started and we've already had three days above forty. It's mad,' she says.

Natasha says, 'It's terrifying.'

I think of Maggie and Mac, boiling like fish in their apartment. I make a mental note to call them.

When we get to the bar, Natasha orders us each an espresso martini.

'So,' she says, taking a seat between Cloudy and me, 'how was it seeing Hugo yesterday?'

'I told you—I'm not talking about him with you.'

'Who's Hugo?' asks Cloudy.

'*Her* brother,' I say, pointing to Natasha.

'They're dating,' Natasha explains.

I roll my eyes.

'Where'd he take you?' Natasha says, leaning in.

'We went on the London Eye and—'

'Ha! Are you serious?' Natasha asks, laughing. 'Hugo is terrified of heights!'

'Yeah. As I soon found out . . .'

She stops laughing, says quietly, 'He must really like you.'

This bar is Natasha's favourite. Red leather and dark wood. Dimly lit, with art adorning every wall and candles wedged in glass bottles at the centre of every table. Cloudy takes our candle and tilts it, dripping wax onto a coaster. With her fingers, she sculpts it into the shape of a hip, a smooth curve. The wax is opalescent in the flickering light.

We finish our drinks and Natasha heads for the bar, returning minutes later with three elderflower cocktails. I take out the skewered lychee, eat it whole. Juice fills my mouth in a burst.

'So do you have any plans for after the show?' Natasha asks Cloudy.

'I'm going to visit an old lover in Berlin,' the artist replies. 'She was my first love, actually.'

'How are you feeling about seeing her?' I ask.

'Nervous,' she says, 'but also excited.'

Natasha asks, 'Could you rekindle the romance?'

Cloudy shakes her head. 'We grew in different directions. But I still feel connected to her.'

I think of Maggie, how she spoke about rivers converging, people flowing together, swirling in great lakes, parting. Meeting again at the river mouth.

'And anyway,' says Cloudy, 'I'm with someone else now. She's electric.'

'Is she an artist too?' I ask.

Cloudy shakes her head. 'Ella's a poet. She says the things I can't say with paint. And I say the things she can't say with words.'

'Sounds perfect,' says Natasha.

'It is,' says Cloudy. 'And the sex is out of this world. When we met, we didn't leave my studio for a week.'

Natasha raises her eyebrows. 'That's impressive.'

'I could live in sex,' Cloudy says, laughing. Natasha joins in.

And in the sound that comes out of me, I try to imagine the walls of Cloudy's sex, because where mine are barbed, hers must be something else.

white sand

For the opening, I wear black trousers, a black turtleneck and a white blazer I found for a pound at the Portobello Road Market. It has shoulder pads that make me look broader than I am. Stronger than I am.

Natasha has given me a cab charge, so that I don't have to catch the tube. It feels decadent and unnecessary. It *is* decadent and unnecessary. *But you have to look the part*, she'd told me.

Though when I arrive, no one is here yet. Look the part for whom?

I step out of the taxi, unlock the gallery, turn on the lights. And a feeling of pride floods my chest. The work looks phenomenal. Cloudy's stormy landscapes. Vivienne's portraits of women who, until now, have largely been written out of history. Holly's sculptures of shapely sandstone bodies, gold strung around their necks. And at the back of the gallery, Mikaela's light installation is a kaleidoscope of colour, refracting around meshed wire. The shape of a woman stretching.

Natasha arrives wearing her usual all-black uniform. 'Where's catering?' she asks.

'They just arrived out back. I told them to start bringing everything in.'

'Good,' she says. Looking around the gallery, she rests her hand on my shoulder. 'I can't wait for everyone to see this.'

I think of Maggie, of the nights when no one came. How brave she'd been. How daring. And I feel myself swelling. Thinking that, even if no one comes, I made this. I saw this.

When Hugo arrives, the gallery is packed. He weaves his way through the crowd, finds my hand. Kisses me on the cheek.

'This is incredible,' he says. 'Congratulations.'

He's wearing my dangly earring.

Natasha finds me at the bar chatting to a client. She waits for us to finish speaking, then says, 'Oli, this is Alison Waite. She's the CEO of Southern Star Expeditions.'

'Hi,' I say, offering her my hand. 'Nice to meet you.'

'Have you heard of us?' she asks.

'I haven't,' I admit, before someone bumps into me, almost spilling my drink.

'Nice save,' she says, then points to the far side of the gallery, where the crowd isn't so dense. 'How about we talk over there?'

We walk over and find a quiet corner in which to stand.

'I haven't heard of Southern Star,' I say. 'Sorry.'

'Not a problem,' she says, smiling. 'We organise expeditions to Antarctica. At the moment I'm working on putting together a group of women artists, musicians and writers to go down there and make work about the changing landscape.'

I think of the Southern Ocean. Vast and undulating.

'Oh . . . amazing,' I mutter, though it's barely audible.

'What was that?' she asks. 'It's hard to hear in here.'

I take a deep breath. 'I said, that sounds amazing.'

'I've been following the women in this show. I'm very impressed.'

The Southern Ocean. Unforgiving.

I finish my wine in one gulp.

At the other end of the gallery, Natasha taps her glass with a cheese knife to silence the crowd.

'Let's talk again later,' Alison suggests.

'Sure,' I say, and make my way through the crowd to join Natasha and our artists.

Natasha thanks everyone for coming, then turns to me. 'And now Oli, who has curated this magnificent show, will say a few words.'

'To reiterate what Natasha said, I'd like to thank you all so much for being here tonight,' I say, my voice quivering with nerves.

Natasha puts her hand on my back and I feel her energy flowing through me. Down into me. I take a deep breath.

'This exhibition was inspired by a woman whom many of you know, either personally or by reputation. I'm speaking, of course, about Maggie Walker. She held one of London's first-ever all-woman shows more than fifty years ago . . . and no one came. But what was important, she told me, was that *she* saw those women. And those women saw each other. Because even as women, we don't always see each other. This exhibition is about spotlight. It's about shining light on work that is diverse and deserving of space. And I'm so thankful to you all for *seeing* this work, and for investing in these women. Because they're not *women* artists.' I raise my glass. 'They are *artists*. Asserting themselves. Unapologetically.'

I look across at Cloudy, Vivienne, Holly and Mikaela. Standing hand in hand, as the crowd raises their glasses. *Seeing* them. In all their glory.

When the formalities are over, Hugo finds me. He tells me my speech was great, that *I'm* great. He tells me I inspire him.

I want to believe it.

The night is bitterly cold. The kind of cold that burns where your skin is exposed. I breathe into my hands, rubbing them together.

Hugo is standing a few metres away with his arm outstretched, trying to hail a cab.

After three cabs drive by without stopping, I spot one coming and step out onto the road, holding my hand up, forcing it to stop.

Hugo grabs my arms and pulls me back onto the footpath as the cab pulls up to the kerb.

'What the hell was that?' he says. 'You could've been run over.'

I ignore him and get into the cab. He follows me in.

'Oli?'

'I knew it was going to stop.'

'No, you didn't,' he says, reaching for my hand, holding it tight. 'Didn't that scare you?'

I shrug. 'Not really.'

'It scared me,' he says.

I look away from him, out the window. And perhaps it's the drink in my belly, or maybe it's the way he's holding my hand—something that makes me blurt out, without thinking, 'I have a feeling I'll die in my twenties.'

'What?' he says.

'I just have a feeling I'll die in my twenties.'

'Well, you might, if you keep doing things like that.'

And I want to ask him, *Why don't I care, Hugo? Why aren't I scared?* But nothing comes out.

There are movies that show you how it happens. The hand-holding in the cab. The giggling walking up the path. The stumbling up the stairs. The way he'll kiss your neck at the front door when you're trying to find your keys. The way your clothes will slide off. How effortless it all is. How effortless it's all *meant* to be.

But there's nothing to tell you how to move your body in the in-between. When you open the front door and wish you'd put the washing away. Because the in-between is the gaps that the films don't show. Where the clothes don't come off effortlessly. When trousers get caught around ankles and the turtleneck almost rips out your earrings. Where you have to actually get *into* those positions. Climbing onto the bed. Sucking in your tummy. Bending your leg in a way you're not sure it actually bends. Knocking heads.

Because it's in those gaps on the cutting-room floor that people fumble and are awkward and smell and say things they don't mean. In the heat of the moment. Things like, *I might be falling in love with you.*

'Me too,' I say. And I want to mean it.

Because now he's climbing off me. Wrapping his body around mine like a silk cocoon. I do. I want to mean it. But as our breathing slows, and the sweat on our bodies begins to cool, there's a distant ache in my side.

I shiver.

'You cold?' he asks, pulling the blanket over us, hugging my body closer.

I shake my head. Because I'm not cold. I'm not anything.

I close my eyes. Squeeze them shut. Feeling his fingers trailing across my back like I am white sand, and he is carving out space for rivers.

I wake when dawn whitens the sky. Hugo is sleeping with his mouth open. Morning breath is hot on my neck. I peel his arm off me, and get out of bed. He's dead asleep. I stand over him, gazing at his body. The curve of his back. A shoulderblade jutting out. His long legs. The tiny patch of hair at the base of his spine. His hand resting between folds of cotton. His bony fingers.

I feel my hands trembling.

He looks huge in my bed. And all I want to do is lie back down. But I want to lie down without him there.

I poke him, whispering, 'Hugo . . . *Hugo*.'

He wakes in a sudden gasp of air.

'Sorry,' I whisper. 'I want to go running.'

He looks at me sleepily. And I think maybe he wants to say, 'I didn't know you ran.' Or, 'Can't I stay here until you get back?' But to my relief, he doesn't say any of those things. He just says, 'Okay. Yeah. That's fine,' and smiles. 'Maybe I'll get in to work early for once.'

I pick up his clothes from the floor and pass them to him. He gets dressed and I think maybe I should put running gear on, but I don't have any, so I just wrap a towel around myself.

We walk together into my living room. And as I'm about to open the front door for him, he says, 'You know, I was thinking about what you said last night . . .'

'What did I say last night?' Though I'm sure I already know what he's referring to.

'About how you think you'll die in your twenties.'

I wrap my arms around myself.

'You dying in your twenties is not romantic,' he says. His eyes are dense black, half in shadow. He shakes his head. 'It would be a waste.'

He crosses the living room, holds my waist with both hands, and kisses my forehead. His lips pressed to my brow, for a long time. I close my eyes. Holding my breath. We choose to breathe, don't we?

Hugo leaves, I close the door, walk into my room and strip the bed. Then I go into the bathroom and get into the shower and throw up.

I scrub my body until it's red and raw, staying in the shower until the water turns cold. The word *waste* swirling on the tiles like an oil slick.

Hugo arrives at the gallery after lunch with a bouquet of flowers. White lilies. Ghosts among the foliage. Like half-opened eyes.

'Here,' he says, handing me the flowers. 'These are for you.'

I take the bouquet. 'They're beautiful.'

He smiles. 'How was your run?'

'My what?'

'Your run this morning?'

Feeling my cheeks redden, I say, 'Oh right . . . yeah. It was good. Though I didn't run very far.' Speaking quietly so that Natasha won't hear me lying to her brother.

violet sand

Hugo and I arrive back at the gallery after a long lunch in Covent Garden. I'm worried Natasha will care how long we've been gone, but when I walk through the door, she's standing by my desk, waving me over.

'Oli,' she says, 'sit down. Sit down.'

'What?' I say. *Sit down?* I feel panic wash over me. Has something happened to Mac? To Maggie?

'I have huge news!' she says.

'Good news?' Hugo asks.

'Yes,' Natasha snaps.

I take a seat at my desk. 'Okay. Fire away.'

'Do you remember Alison Waite?'

'Who?'

'She was at the opening. I introduced the two of you.'

'You introduced me to a lot of people.'

'She's the CEO of Southern Star Expeditions.'

I feel my body stiffen. 'The Antarctica lady?'

'*Yes*, that one.'

'What does she want?'

'Well,' says Natasha, 'do you remember she told you about an expedition she was organising for women artists, writers, musicians . . . ?'

'Yeah, I think so.'

'She wants you to curate the show when they all get back from Antarctica.'

'Really?' I ask.

'Yeah! And that's not even the best part!'

I laugh. 'What is then?'

'She wants you to go with them on the expedition.'

'What?'

'She wants you to go to Antarctica!'

'How?'

'On a boat! From South America!' she exclaims.

Hugo interjects, 'No way! How cool is that?'

'No,' I say, shaking my head. 'Tell her no.'

'What?' says Natasha, dumbfounded.

I look down at the polished concrete and imagine it turning to water. I imagine the gallery flooding. Water stretching until it's here. There. Everywhere. All around, for miles and miles.

I feel the earth rocking. It's all back and forth. Back and forth.

'Sorry. But my answer is no,' I say, and excuse myself for the bathroom.

Later, as I'm stepping out of the shower, my phone starts to ring. I rush to answer it, seeing that the number is Australian, but my fingers are wet, and the touch screen won't read wet hands. The phone rings out. I dry my hands and return the call.

Maggie picks up on the second ring. 'Hello, my love,' she says. Her voice is croaky, though I feel a smile widening on hearing it. My entire being seems to fill out.

'Hey, Maggie.'

'How was your show?' she asks.

'Good. Really good,' I say, beaming. 'I have the exhibition brochure to post to you.'

'Yes! Please do!'

'How are you?'

'Oh, don't you worry about that,' she says, 'I'm calling for a more important reason.'

'Oh yeah—like what?' I ask.

Maggie starts coughing. The deep kind of cough that makes you wince with sympathy. I hear Mac talking in the background. Something about water, and calling back later. 'No, no,' I hear her say between coughs. Her voice elsewhere in the room. 'I'm fine.'

I wait until she returns to the phone.

'Natasha tells me you've been offered a gig in Antarctica.'

I feel the air rush out of me. 'Well. Potentially.'

'You know,' she croaks, 'I have this idea, that all the souls in the world return to the Antarctic . . . It's the oldest river mouth . . . I like to think that Robynne is there . . . That she went home.'

I say nothing.

'Oh, Oli,' she says at last, 'you have to go!'

'I can't,' I say. 'Maggie . . . I just can't.'

gold sand

For a while, time passes effortlessly.

Just like that. The sky widens. The days become longer. And I don't mind. Because this love grows around me like green after fire, so that my body is no longer exposed. With Hugo, the openness of light is bearable. Magnolias bloom. Petals pepper the ground. Soft under feet, as we walk barefoot through Regent's Park.

At sunset, we lie together beneath a cherry blossom, a canopy of pink.

'It's almost blue time,' whispers Hugo.

I roll onto my side, facing him now. His breath light on my cheek.

'Blue time?'

'Yeah,' he says, smiling. 'It's when the sun sets and everything takes on a blue tinge . . .' Hugo touches my lips, my jaw. He brushes my hair back off my face, cradling my head in the palm of his hand. I close my eyes as he draws me closer. And then he's kissing me. Gently. As the sun dips beneath the trees, and we sink into blue.

He laughs.

'What?'

'I don't know,' he says. 'It's stupid.'

I smile, watching his cheeks flush pink. 'Tell me.'

'You're just, like, the coolest thing that's ever happened to me.'

And now I'm laughing too. For a moment, forgetting the part of me that wants to say, *If only you knew.*

Outside my bedroom window, tiny yellow buds open into stars. Every morning when I wake, there are more of them, these flowers. And I notice that with each new bloom, I show more of myself. I leave the door open to the bathroom when I get changed so that he can keep talking to me. Eventually, I stop getting changed in the bathroom at all.

I peel off my top, wriggle out of my trousers, and unhook my bra, letting it fall on the floor. Slowly, I slide off my underwear and, as it lands at my ankles, I look up at him. Hugo's lying on my bed in sweatpants. Propped up on a pillow, he looks at me with smiling eyes. His gaze drifting across my skin like clouds across the sky.

Looking down at my body, I remember that someone told me once, *You're not* that *thin.* And how, with my bones jutting out at sharp angles, I'd harboured those words. Believing in them. Always returning to them like a prayer before sleep.

Then I think of arriving here in London with Maggie, after I'd spent a month in her bed in Sydney, unable to move, unable to speak. How viciously the cold had seized me when we stepped off the plane. How much it all had hurt. And how when Maggie and Lindy finally got me eating again, I'd gradually gained weight. How, for the first time in my life, I didn't mind that the gap between my thighs was closing, or that my belly was rounding, or that my arms were thickening. Because this extra weight became a fleshy armour that protected me, protected my secret. My flesh made me feel safe.

Still, I avoided mirrors. And because no one ever saw me in this body, I could exist in it. Until no one became *Hugo*. And, suddenly, my flesh felt overwhelming.

'Come here,' he says.

I step forwards, leaving my underwear on the floor. He rolls onto his back, arms outstretched. I climb onto the bed, my breath shallow to hold in my belly. He whispers, 'You're incredible,' and as my breath escapes, I relax my tummy muscles and lie down beside him. He brushes his fingers across my flesh, the curve of my hip, the pink of my thigh. His touch raises goosebumps on my skin. 'I fucking adore you,' he says. And there's a lump in my throat. But then he's kissing me, moving his body above mine. Kissing the hollow of my neck, my collarbones, my breasts, my belly. The insides of my thighs. His tongue. And then his fingers, slow and gentle. Touching me. Until I'm closing my eyes and sinking back. My thighs begin to quiver.

And soon, it's as if he's pouring liquid gold into me, because I can feel the warmth of it spreading through my abdomen, flowing down into my legs. My muscles clench around him, my body beginning to spasm. It's a sensation I've never felt before. Like my entire body is filling now. Filling. Full.

But then a sound escapes me and my eyes burst open. And I see the shock on his face, his eyes wide, his mouth gaping. I cover my mouth with my hands, muffling my gasp. Hoping he didn't hear. But he did. His face is twisting as he tries to suppress his laughter. 'Don't laugh at me!' I cry.

'I'm not!' he says, and presses his lips together, trying so hard not to giggle.

'You are!' I turn over onto my side, unable to look at him.

'It's just a fart, Oli!' he says, laughing out loud now. 'I don't care! Honestly!'

Mortified, I pull my knees up to my chest, curling into a ball. 'I just want to roll into a hole and die,' I mumble.

He curves his body around mine. 'Well,' he says, 'make sure there's room in there for two.'

And I realise that, like the yellow buds outside flowering into stars, it's impossible not to open when someone loves every inch of you.

yellow sand

Summer arrives and the papers talk about the heatwave. All the parks have yellowed, flowers folding in on themselves. 'Terrifying,' says Hugo. Again, and again. 'Just terrifying.'

We meet Natasha at Paddington one Saturday in June. We're sipping black coffee at the station when she arrives. Hugo is holding my hand across the table. 'Oh, you two!' she says, approaching us. 'My heart!'

I roll my eyes and Hugo laughs.

'I didn't know you had a heart,' he says and she pinches his ear.

I look at my watch. 'Better get moving.'

Hugo downs the rest of his coffee in one mouthful. He winces. Coughs. 'Fuck,' he says. 'I should not have done that!'

Natasha laughs. 'Your IQ baffles me.'

'Yeah, yeah,' he says. 'Come on, let's go. Jules will kill us if we miss this train.'

On the train to Oxford, Hugo tells me again about his little sister's work. I hear: *lasers . . . gases . . . camera . . . atoms exploding!* 'It's so cool,' he says, glowing with pride. 'Like, it's completely new! No one's ever done it before.'

I touch Hugo's cheek, and he quietens. 'Sorry,' he says sheepishly. 'Too much info?'

'No, no,' I say, giggling, 'I just don't get it.'

I think of the first time Hugo told me about his younger sister, how he'd said she was studying physical chemistry and I thought that meant she was studying *love*. I remember how hard he'd tried not to laugh.

'Don't worry,' Natasha says, 'it's another language to me as well.'

'Jules is definitely our mum's favourite,' says Hugo.

Natasha shoots him a sharp glance. 'Only because she's the youngest.'

Hugo whispers in my ear, 'She's just jealous.'

'You're not very good at whispering, *Hugo*,' snaps Natasha.

I kiss Hugo and turn to face the window, pressing my cheek against the cool glass. Beyond, the fields are bleached, like bone coral.

Hugo is looking out as well now, but he doesn't comment. He just sighs. The colour of the air leaving him is a painful yellow.

Julia meets us at the station. Hugo points her out, though he hardly needs to. She's just like him. Tall and lanky with tortoiseshell glasses, a plaid miniskirt and a t-shirt that reads, *There is no PLAN-et B. Period.*

'Oli!' She throws her arms around me. 'Finally!' She steps back, smiling. 'I've heard *so* much about you,' she says, pointing to Hugo. 'Oh my God. He literally won't shut up about you! Oli, Oli, I love Oli sooo—'

Hugo reaches across and covers her mouth with his hand. 'And this is Jules!' he says, his face bright red.

I blow him a kiss.

'I'm so happy you're here!' Jules says, hugging her siblings.

'You're looking well,' Natasha says.

'So what's the plan?' Hugo asks.

Jules looks at me; I'm fanning my face with the newspaper Hugo brought with us on the train. 'Well, I was going to suggest we show Oli the colleges before lunch, but maybe we can go up to the river first? Do you have swimmers?'

'I don't swim,' says Natasha.

Jules pokes her tongue out at her older sister. 'Oli?'

I shake my head. 'I'm keen to see the colleges, though.'

'Okay, then!' she says, clapping her hands together. 'How about we see my college first?'

'Perfect,' I say.

Hugo touches my back, smoothing my shirt with the palm of his hand. I can feel the fabric dampening between my shoulderblades. 'You okay?'

I nod.

'Sure?'

I'm thinking of the water, the body of it, like a snake.

'Yeah,' I say, and feign a smile. 'I'm fine.'

Hugo takes my hand as we follow Jules out of the station. 'Worcester is only five minutes away,' says Jules. Outside, the light is harsh. I hold Hugo's hand a little tighter and he smiles. Jules points out the SAID Business School and explains that the university buildings are dotted all around the city. We turn a corner beneath a magnolia tree. The sun is sticky on my neck.

'And here we are!' she says, opening her arms out wide. 'Ta-da!'

'Wow,' I say, gazing up. The clock on the wall above us is full and round. Opalescent like the moon.

We follow Jules through the front gates and into a quadrangle with perfectly mown grass. On the right is a mighty building with high arched windows and strings of ivy that spread out across the sandstone like veins beneath skin. Flowers are in full bloom. Tangles of pink and blue.

On the left is a building with a grey, wrinkled face. Jules tells us it's medieval as we walk through its tunnel, Hugo ducking his head to avoid bumping it on the low ceiling. The tunnel opens out onto a sprawling lawn rimmed with tulips and roses. In its centre are three oak trees, sunlight falling through the withered leaves. We pass beneath their canopy, walking through a shower of gold. Beyond them, the path widens at the edge of a lake. On the far bank I see two swans.

A laugh escapes me. 'I cannot believe this is your backyard . . . It's stunning!'

'I know,' says Jules. 'I'm so lucky.'

'Don't say that,' says Hugo. 'You worked your butt off to get here.'

'I'm not saying I didn't work hard,' she says. 'I mean, fuck, I'm the only woman in my group. But I'm also white, and this place was built for white people.'

Hugo says, 'True,' and we keep walking, passing beneath a stone archway laced with vines to a tree that overhangs the lake. There are two students sitting in its branches, reading.

I'm still thinking about what Jules has said about the place being built for white people and ask her what she meant by it.

'Well, it's not like the university says it only wants white people, or doesn't want people of colour. Like, it's not just someone standing at the front door saying you can come in and you can't. It's the thousand obstacles along the street that stop a person from even reaching the house.'

I try to imagine what obstacles might exist along the street, but find myself unable to picture the shape of something I haven't seen. And in that absence of understanding, that inability to picture, I realise, my *knowing* is incomplete. The realisation of this *beyond,* of something outside my experience, is painfully obvious, and yet it still feels shocking.

I admit to Jules, 'I've never really thought much about being white.'

Jules shrugs. 'I guess that's what privilege is.'

We have lunch at a market across the road from Jules's college and then walk through the centre of the town, past the Bodleian Library to University Church. All around, students pedal bicycles, sailing casually around corners with summer ease.

Paying four pounds, we ascend the stairs of the church. The climb is steep and the walls tight, all the way up to a balcony so narrow we have to walk out single file. Hugo is gripping my hand so hard I can feel my blood pulsing in my fingertips. I look over my shoulder to see him with his eyes squeezed shut. I wedge myself between him and the edge of the balcony. 'Hey,' I say, resting my palm on his cheek. He opens one eye.

'Just us,' I say.

He smiles. And then I kiss him and feel his muscles relax. He hugs me close and I turn around in his arms so that I'm facing the sky. In the distance, beyond the spires and tiled roofs, is a string of clouds, lilac at the edges. Hugo rests his chin on my shoulder and whispers in my ear, 'Just us.'

On the walk to Port Meadow, Jules grabs two swimsuits, towels and a picnic rug from her house. Heat from the sun is dense. Sweat gathers between my breasts. I can feel myself wilting.

When we reach the meadow, Jules says in her three years living in Oxford, she's never seen it this colour. The field stretches far back to distant woods. Yellow, like desert sand. I notice a dead bird between tufts of grass. Its feathers are matted and dusty.

'This is my home away from home,' Jules says, as she unfolds the picnic rug and spreads it out on the riverbank. Natasha takes off her shoes and sits down on the rug. Before us is a small river, rimmed with wildflowers, that flows into the Thames downstream. A wooden bridge stretches across the water where the two rivers meet. Children climb up onto its railing, squealing and laughing when they jump off. On the far bank, older teenagers are sunbathing and smoking. Someone is playing music. I'm breathing in short, sharp breaths.

Beside me, Jules wraps a towel around her to change into her swimsuit. Hugo kicks off his shoes then takes off his shirt and his jeans, so that he's standing there in his boxers and a pair of odd socks. Natasha smirks and looks away. Jules laughs and calls him a dork. But he doesn't flinch. Catching my eye, he grins. And in this moment, the hard edges fray. I do love you, I think.

'Oli,' Jules says, waving a swimsuit in front of me.

'Oh,' I mutter. 'Um . . .'

She passes it to me and I notice my hands are shaking. I hold the bathing suit against my torso, my gaze landing on the water.

The river. Like a wound opening up. Dark as an abyss.

I feel myself backing away from the bank.

'Come on,' Hugo says, teasing. 'You're not scared of the water, are you?' He tugs on the swimsuit playfully.

'Don't,' I tell him, pushing his hand away.

Jules steps towards me and asks in a hushed voice, 'Can you swim, Oli?'

I shrug.

Hugo, softer now, touches my upper arm and whispers in my ear, 'Just us . . .' He smiles. 'You don't have to be embarrassed.'

'I'm not embarrassed!' I snap.

Quietly, he says my name.

'Don't touch me.'

Hugo recoils, visibly hurt. And I want to say something. *Anything.* But my words are half-formed things. Like smoke changing shape. Suffocating.

'Oli,' says Natasha, tapping her hand on the ground beside her. 'Here—sit down with me, okay?'

I collapse down onto the rug and pull my knees up to my chest, holding my legs together, squeezing them tight. Closing. Shutting. Shutting up.

Hugo crouches down beside me and Natasha waves him away.

'Come on,' says Jules, pulling on her brother's arm.

He stares at me, into me, searching. I turn away.

'Come on, Hugo,' I hear Jules say again. 'Just give her a minute.'

I close my eyes. He sighs, and then he walks away. His footsteps fading pale blue.

purple sand

We never talk about the river. Hugo assumes I can't swim and that I'm deeply embarrassed about it, which is so much easier than anything else. Because how do you explain skin burning to someone who hasn't known fire?

It rains. I keep quiet. Hours seep into days. Leaves discolour. I keep quiet. And the leaves begin to fall. Falling and falling until the ground is muddy purple. Darkness descends, and I can breathe.

In November, a cold snap moves in from the east. The wind is bitter grey, and as we walk out of the station at London Bridge, a gust of it grabs hold of me. Full-bodied. I let it. Let it hold me. Painfully tight. Because these edges are thin. And more and more often, I feel how porous my borders are. All those holes in my flesh. Like parts of me are seeping out. Into everything. Into nothing.

Above me, the sky is mottled with bruises. Hugo is walking a few feet ahead. He turns and asks, 'What does he look like?'

I think of the last time I saw Will, the summer he finished high school. I'd been home for a few weeks before Christmas, packing up the rest of the apartment in Manly so my father could sell it. I'd been between yacht deliveries and, since my father was still furious that I'd given up an internship to pursue a life at sea, I'd spent Christmas morning with Will and Annie before lunch at Mac and Maggie's. By New Year's Eve I'd found work on another boat, *King Tide*, and was sailing out the heads.

I shrug. 'It's been so long.' And for a moment, gazing out into the sea of faces, I think: *He could be anyone.* But then I spy him, across the road. Hand in hand with his love. And my lips curve into a smile.

I wave and he waves back. Beaming.

The green light for pedestrians flashes and Will hurries across the road. Reaching us, he lets go of his boyfriend's hand and throws his arms around me. He's even taller than I remember. Long and lean, with bleached hair, a gold earring and a tattoo of a rose on his neck. Our embrace is honest warmth and I can feel the years between us dissolving.

He steps back, and says, 'Oli, this is Ramos.'

'It's so nice to finally meet you!' I say, and then introduce Hugo.

'Shall we head to the restaurant then?' asks Hugo.

Will nods. 'I'm freezing!'

As we walk, I ask Will and Ramos, 'So how's the trip going?'

'Amazing,' says Ramos.

'I just loved Paris!' adds Will.

They describe their stay in the eleventh arrondissement with a friend from art school. How they'd gone to galleries every day. Dressed themselves in vintage clothes from one-euro bins. Walked the Seine. Broken their budget on rosé and three-course meals. Had a picnic under the Eiffel Tower, the ground carpeted with orange leaves. Partied in a laneway.

'It sounds wonderful,' I say as we arrive at the restaurant. 'I'm so happy for you.'

Inside the heating is on full bore. We strip off our top layers, hanging our coats on a rack, and Hugo comments that the heat is unnecessary.

The restaurant is walled with white tiles, black grout between. Plants hanging from the ceiling. Natasha is already at the table with a bottle of wine and five glasses. 'This is my boss, Natasha.'

She rolls her eyes. 'I'm not your boss right now.'

'It's so great to meet you,' Will gushes. 'We've been following your gallery for, well, like, ever.'

'Oh,' says Natasha. 'Thank you. That's nice to hear.'

Hugo pours the wine as a waiter hands us menus, and I ask Will and Ramos about their art. Ramos explains how his photographic practice has changed since graduating, now that he no longer has access to a darkroom and his negatives are developed by someone else.

'It's created a distance, I think, in my work . . . I have less control.'

'Still,' says Will, 'your work is unbelievable.' He turns to me. 'Here, look at this,' he says, pulling out his phone. The lock screen is a photo of two naked bodies, contorted. So abstract you can't tell where the limbs extend from. There are no beginnings. And no ends.

'Wow,' I whisper.

Natasha lowers her menu. 'Show me,' she says. And Ramos's muscles clench, his body stiffening. Natasha ponders the work a moment in silence. I guess from Ramos's face that this silence is painful and intimidating, but I know it's a good sign. If Natasha wasn't interested, she'd have already looked away.

At last, she says, 'Yes . . .' and Ramos's face lights up. 'Very impressive.' Then she looks at Will. 'And what about your work?'

'I'm a performance artist,' he says. 'Mostly I combine body paint and movement. I love the idea that my canvas is breathing.'

'It's really something,' says Ramos. 'We'd been at art school together for a year, but hadn't met. We were studying in different departments—'

Will interrupts him. 'But then Ramos saw me perform,' he says theatrically, flicking his fringe away from his face, 'and the rest is history.'

Ramos laughs. Shrugs. 'It's true.'

I smile. 'Have you ever collaborated on a show?'

'That's the dream, isn't it?'

Will nods. 'We've always wanted to, but straight out of art school, we've found it hard to get a space.'

'Perhaps I'll have to get you back over here soon,' I say. 'I'd like to see the interplay of the still body in the photos and the live body in performance.'

Both of them are beaming and without words.

Finally, Will says, 'We read about your first all-woman show.'

'Ah, yes,' I say. 'I was really happy with it. Their work looked phenomenal.'

'We've been following Vivienne's work for a few years now.'

'She's brilliant, isn't she?'

'And so open about her transition,' says Will. 'We know a lot of young people who really look up to her.'

'It was actually her first time exhibiting since her affirmation surgery,' I say. 'I felt honoured to show her.'

'Amazing,' says Ramos.

'Did your parents go to the opening?' Will asks me.

I shake my head. 'I invited them.'

'Fuck,' says Will.

'My dad hardly spoke to me for years after I ditched that internship.'

'But you're doing so well now . . .'

'He's never taken art seriously.'

Hugo holds my hand under the table, gently squeezing it.

'I found out later that he was actually in London the week of the show.'

'Brutal,' says Will.

'Oh well. Mum is coming to visit me in February. That will be interesting.'

Will laughs. 'Parents . . .'

'We thought mine were cool with us,' says Ramos, 'but just before we left we heard them tell my family back in the Philippines that I'm going on a holiday with my *best friend*.'

Will puts his arm around Ramos's shoulder and says, 'I *am* your best friend.'

Ramos smiles, but it's tinged with sadness. Blue at the edges.

'I love you,' says Will, and kisses him on the cheek.

'How was Annie?' I ask. 'When you told her, I mean.'

'Not great, to be honest.'

'*Really?*' I say, shocked. 'She's always struck me as very progressive.'

'She is,' he says. 'And she has so many gay friends.'

'What was the problem then?'

'She said that she was worried people would discriminate against me if I chose to live this life.' He's looking at the table now, playing with his napkin. 'What she didn't realise was that she was the only one giving me grief about it.'

'And she thinks it's a choice,' I say.

'Exactly. That probably hurt the most.'

A waiter approaches the table. 'Are you ready to order?'

'Get whatever you want,' I say to Will and Ramos. 'This one's on me.'

They glance at each other, unsure. '*Really?*' Will asks.

'Of course,' I say.

We each order our dishes. The waiter leaves, Natasha tops up our glasses, and then Hugo says, '*Mothers . . .*' and Natasha very nearly spits out her wine. '*What?*' says Natasha.

'Maybe I shouldn't generalise . . .'

'No,' she snaps. 'You shouldn't.'

'Fine,' Hugo says, and I don't know if he's just trying to contribute to a conversation that he feels outside of, but when he adds, '*Our* mother certainly said some crazy things,' my body recoils. Like a tiny creature into its shell. And I feel myself. Behind a wooden door. In the dark. Wet. Rocking back and forth. Noise filtering through. *She's fucking crazy.*

'You think our mum is crazy?'

'I didn't say that.'

'You implied it.'

'You're putting words in my mouth.'

'Am I?'

Ramos and Will have put their glasses down. Will looks at me, his mouth ajar. He's waiting for me to say something. But I can't. I can't say anything at all.

'I feel like you're attacking me,' says Hugo.

'*Attacking* you?' Natasha says, her words razor-sharp. 'You just said something problematic.'

I swallow and feel it, my saliva thick in my throat.

'I don't get why it's such a big deal.'

'Hmm,' says Natasha, 'maybe because you've just suggested that the woman who raised you, *single-handedly*, occasionally got a little "crazy".'

Hugo shrugs. 'Now you're acting crazy.'

Natasha flinches. 'Yeah? *Am I?* Or am I just pissed off that that's the bullshit kind of thing our dad used to say to undermine her for years before he fucked off.'

'And,' I say quietly, noise filtering through, 'women have been locked up for being crazy.'

'Exactly! Thank you, Oli.' Natasha flicks her hair back off her face. 'Do you get that, Hugo?'

He mumbles something, barely audible.

'What?'

'I'm sorry,' he says.

'It's a loaded word, okay?'

'I guess. I've never thought about it like that before.'

Will musters a smile and says kindly, 'We're all on our own journey.'

'Will's right,' Natasha concedes. She rubs Hugo's shoulder. 'It's okay—we're all learning.'

I take a deep breath, turn to Will and, as if the last few minutes haven't happened, ask, 'Does she get it now? Your mum, I mean.'

'Yeah,' he says, 'it took a while. But once I realised it was coming from a place of love, we became closer than ever. Like, she really understands now that this is just who I am—and she adores Ramos.'

'That's great,' I say, as our food is set down in front of us.

As we eat Natasha asks Will and Ramos where they're headed next and they discuss their travel plans. Hugo's leg brushes mine under the table.

I edge away, and he says nothing. He just sits in silence, hunched over his meal, until we've finished lunch and are out on the street saying goodbye to Will and Ramos. Quietly, he wishes them safe travels, kisses Natasha on the cheek, and then turns to me. I sidestep him and start walking.

'Oli,' he says. 'Oli, wait up.'

I power ahead to the station.

Hugo catches me at the top of the stairs. 'Oli.' He grabs my hand. 'I'm sorry, okay? I said something stupid. I didn't know what it meant. Not really. But now I do.' He gives my hand a squeeze. 'I'm learning. I really am.'

I look up.

His eyes are searching for me. Deep brown with green frills. And as his gaze settles on mine, it's painful. Because he sees me. He really sees me. In sharp focus. And I'm terrified. Thinking, *What does he see? What can he know?*

By the time we get back to my apartment, my fingers are numb. Hugo tells me that my lips are purple and says he'll run me a bath. I make myself a cup of tea in the kitchen, wrapping my hands around the mug to warm them. Slowly, sensation is restored in tingles shaped like tiny stars.

Hugo returns from the bathroom and says, 'It's ready.'

I follow him into a room of quiet shadows. Candlelight dances across the tiles. I breathe in. Sandalwood is orange on my tongue. There are dried rose petals on the water, uncurling as they soak through. Pink blooming into blood red. I begin undressing. Hugo, leaning against the doorframe, watches in silence as I peel away each layer.

I slide my underwear down and step out of it. He turns away.

'Aren't you getting in?' I ask.

He looks up, half smiling. 'I didn't know if you wanted me to . . .'

'Please,' I say, and he steps onto the tiles, raising his arms. I take his jumper from his hips and pull it up to his neck. 'You're too tall!' I say, laughing now. 'You do it!'

He smiles sheepishly and pulls it over his head. Then he wriggles out of his jeans and takes off his socks so that we're both here, in half-shadows. Breathing softly. He steps closer, so that our naked torsos are pressing together, holds my face gently between his palms and whispers, 'I love you *so* much.'

Like a mountain river rushing white over granite, those words smooth the hard edges. Slowly, over time and with enough repetition, they'll wear me away to nothing.

Hugo gets into the bath. I climb in and sit between his legs, my spine against his torso. He wraps his arms around me, resting his chin on my shoulder. I begin to thaw. Warmth returning to my bones.

'You okay?' he whispers in my ear.

'Yeah. Why?'

'You're breathing funny.'

'Am I?' I say, feigning surprise. 'I guess it's just hot in here.'

Hugo releases his hold on me. I feel the wetness where his skin had touched mine cooling instantly. I shiver. 'No,' I mumble. 'Hold me.'

He does, but it's not enough.

'Tighter,' I say.

'Are you sure you're okay?'

I nod. Saying nothing. Because I'm looking at the rose petals, delicate on the surface, but my mind is already beneath. Below the waterline. In the dark wet. Thinking about my skin. And his skin. And how, right now, it's flaking off. A constellation of dirt and dead flesh. These bits of skin, scattered like fish scales in a pool of blood.

'Tighter,' I whisper.

grey sand

We drive to Brighton in a car Hugo has rented for the weekend. Why he chose the beach in January, I don't know, but as we leave the city, and the spaces between buildings grow into fields, I'm just thankful to be driving with him into openness.

Hugo holds my hand, even though the car is a manual. He has to let go each time he changes gears before returning, always, to my lap, where he curls his hand around mine.

We stop at a petrol station to fill up with fuel and stock up on road trip food. Back on the highway, I feed him chocolates, and laugh at the childlike way he gobbles them up from my hand.

We drive in silence. And it's not awkward. I'm not searching for words. Because for now, this is perfect.

Hugo booked the apartment we've rented for the weekend, so I'm surprised to discover it's on the beachfront, with huge glass windows facing the sea.

'Wow!' Hugo exclaims, putting the keys down on the table. 'What a view!'

'Yeah,' I say, dropping my bags at my feet. Averting my gaze from the water. 'Should we go down to the promenade? Maybe pick up some food to make dinner with?'

'Sure,' he says, unzipping his bag, 'but first, I have something for you.'

'What is it?'

He pulls a wrapped gift from his bag. Brown paper with a thin blue ribbon.

'I thought we agreed no presents!'

'*You* said no presents,' he says with a smile, offering me the gift.

'But I haven't got you anything.'

'Meh, my birthday was last month,' he says, waving his hand dismissively.

'I'm not thirty *yet*,' I say, reluctantly taking the present, untying the ribbon and peeling off the wrapping paper to reveal a book. *Collected Poems* by Marianne Moore.

'Have you read her before?' he asks.

I shake my head, feeling myself well up.

'Are you okay?' he says.

I nod. 'More than okay.'

He puts his arms around me and the book. I feel its spine

digging into my torso. Only the slight pain of it feels distant, as if in another time.

'I'm happier than I remember being,' he says. His words are skin and bone.

And I am air.

We walk along the promenade, all the way to the pier. Bulbs spelling BRIGHTON PIER lit up gold against a brooding sky. Hugo is holding my hand. He steers me towards the pier. Waves are lapping at its posts. Beyond, swells are rolling like bodies turning over beneath a blanket. 'Come on,' he says. 'There're rides down here.'

We begin to walk from solid concrete onto the pier. Slats of wood. Through the gaps, I see the ocean. Washing back and forth. Sways of white foam. My breath quickens. I taste the salt. Feel it in me. Until suddenly, I can't breathe. My muscles clench like ice snapped frozen. I pull back on Hugo's hand.

'What's wrong?' he asks.

'I don't feel very well,' I mumble.

'Do you feel sick?'

'I don't know.'

'You look like you've seen a ghost.'

'I'm just cold,' I lie. 'Can we go home?'

'Of course,' he says, and we begin walking back into the main part of town. On the way we pass two fishermen. One is reeling in. A fish hooked on a line. Dragged through the water, yanked up onto grey sand.

On the way home, we find a grocery store, buy some vegetables, tofu and green curry paste and take it all home with us.

In the kitchen, I chop carrots and broccoli. Hugo is wearing a beanie with a pompom, loose pants, a woollen jumper and my dangly earring. He's cutting up the tofu and courgettes, sneaking across to my bench from time to time to steal pieces of carrot. I pinch his ear playfully. 'There'll be none left for the curry.'

He laughs and steals another piece, putting it in his mouth before I can snatch it back.

We eat dinner on the couch. The night outside is so thick the sea disappears into blackness. I breathe a sigh of relief.

'Should we watch a movie?' Hugo suggests.

'Sure,' I say. 'Your choice.'

Hugo puts on a cheesy rom-com and I fall asleep before anything really happens.

I wake up to his lips on my cheek. 'Come on,' he whispers, scooping me up. 'Time for bed.'

I wake to a mackerel sky, tiny white clouds spread out like fish scales. The sea is wide and washed grey. I roll away from it and see Hugo has put my present on my bedside table. I pick up the book and open to a random page. 'A Grave.'

A shiver ripples across my skin, raising it like waves rising out of the deep. I read aloud. But with each new sentence, I feel the words thickening. Becoming more solid. They wedge in my throat like blocks of ice.

I put the book down, feel the weight of it pressing on my belly.

Hugo rolls over, kisses my cheek.

I smile and kiss him on the lips. He lifts his hands from under the covers, holds my face. Kissing. Softly at first. Then deeper. Kissing my neck. My breasts. My stomach. He holds my hips. Gently rolling me over. So now I'm facing the windows. Facing the sea. Feeling him feel his way inside me. Softly at first. Then deeper.

And it feels good. It does. Until it doesn't. Because I'm looking at the sea, a well-excavated grave. And imagining all the creatures that have died in it. The seabed an underwater cemetery where flesh stretches and breaks apart. Becomes silt and sand. Grey sand. Made of fish eyes and pieces of skin and bones and scales.

And suddenly, I'm falling water. Under water. Below the surface. Below deck. Stretching for someone. Ripping apart. I feel AJ's hand on my thigh. I freeze. All my muscles, clenching around bone. So hard and so tight, I think my bones might break. Turn into silt and sand. Grey sand. A sky made of fish scales.

Fish guts. Raining down from the heavens. A body. Remembering. Why didn't you just scream?

The body always remembers.

'Oli?

I look over my shoulder. I'm shaking, hyperventilating. I see Hugo. His face washed white.

'Oli? What's wrong?' He's panicked. 'I'm sorry!' he says. 'Whatever I did, I'm sorry.'

He pulls out of me. But I still feel him. Inside. In there. I hold onto my belly. Roll into a ball. Rocking back and forth. It's all back and forth.

Hugo wraps his body around mine. 'I'm sorry, Oli,' he says. 'I'm sorry.'

He holds me until I'm still. Until I can breathe. Until I say, 'I can't be with you.'

And then he lets go.

blue sand

Hugo fades from my life like a scar. Pink turning into white. So that even as the days turn into weeks, I still see him on my skin every time I undress.

At the gallery, Natasha has stopped asking what happened. No more *whys*. It's a relief, because I don't have any answers.

Today, she's already in when I arrive. 'Have you checked your emails?' she asks.

I put her coffee down on her desk. 'Nope,' I say. 'Why?'

'Remember Alison Waite, the one who's planning the Antarctica trip?'

I cast my mind back a year. Mutter, 'Yeah—why?'

'Well, the expedition is next month, and the curator who took it on when you turned it down has had to pull out. Health reasons or something.'

I feel my body contract.

'They still want you.'

I shake my head.

'Oli, this will be huge for you!' says Natasha, adding, 'I've already told her you'll think about it.'

Without Hugo, my weekends are long and drawn out. I become a tourist, trying to spend as little time in my apartment as possible. One weekend it's Tate Britain. The next it's Any Amount of Books. This weekend it's the National Gallery.

From my home in Bethnal Green, I take the Central line to Holborn, then the Piccadilly line to Leicester Square. The sky is ashen, the rain falling in that way I've become so used to: a drizzle so fine the droplets catch in my hair, and land on my cheeks with the slightest touch. Despite the rain, a street performer is still presenting his act to a cluster of children in plastic ponchos. I feel in my pockets for change, find a pound coin and toss it in his hat. Inside the gallery I shed my layers, leaving my scarf, gloves and winter coat in the cloakroom.

For hours, I wander through rooms with blood-red walls and polished floors. My limbs heavy. A distant ache. Sleepwalking. Until a certain picture wakes me up.

It's Piero del Pollaiuolo's *Apollo and Daphne*. A portrait of a man, swollen with desire. Engorged. And a woman, turning into a tree. Becoming something else. Her outstretched arms, wooden. Sprouting leaves. One leg, rippled bark. Rooted to the earth. She can't move.

I know this story.

And I want to look away. Because there's a growing pain in my side. Piercing purple. Muscle remembering. But I can't. I can't take my eyes off her.

I can't take my eyes off his thigh, riding up under hers. Between her legs. Spreading her legs. Opening her up. His hands, wrapped around her hips. Holding her down. Her eyes, half open. Caught in a dream. A dreamy romance. A nightmare. The Freeze.

I can hear her screaming. *Is this really happening?*

I stumble backwards, collapse onto the couch in the middle of the room. Blood dripping from the walls. Plush leather. A dead animal. I shudder.

As, for the first time in years, the clouds open above the desert. And I feel my eyes watering. Blink.

Tears fall out of me like rain. Filling all the rivers he'd carved out.

silver sand

I arrive at my mum's hotel in Covent Garden just before twelve. Its exterior is white walls and sculpted hedges. At the hotel's entrance are wide glass doors with gold trimmings. A man in a suit opens the door for me. 'Welcome,' he says.

At reception I tell the man behind the desk that I'm meeting Laura Winters. 'One moment,' he says, picking up the phone to call her room. 'You can wait over there.' He points to a lounge by a huge window that overlooks a courtyard with white-and-black-chequered tiles. Fairy lights nestled between foliage. A man and woman are sipping glasses of red at a nearby table.

'Sparkling wine?' offers a woman carrying a tray of champagne flutes.

'I'm fine, thank you.'

A moment later, the lift doors open and my mother steps out. Her silk dress is the colour of pink pearls. Over it, she wears a long black coat. I stand to greet her. And as I put my arms around her, I feel the sharpness with which her spine protrudes. She's the thinnest she's ever been.

Still, her make-up is immaculate. Supple red lips. Dark lashes. Gold lids. And from her ears hang silver hoops so thick and heavy they make her earlobes sag. She looks like a painting. And then I realise that she looks like a painting not because of her perfectly applied make-up, but because of her eyes. There's no light in them.

She looks past me, around the foyer, and then says, 'So where is he?'

'Who?'

'Your boyfriend.'

'What?'

'Hugo.'

'Oh, right, yeah,' I mumble, remembering that the last time we spoke at any length was Christmas. 'He's not coming.'

'Why not?'

'We broke up.'

'You what?'

'We broke up, Mum. We're not together anymore.'

'But I came all this way to meet him,' she says.

I pause. Then bite back. 'And to see me.'

'Oh, you know that's not what I meant.'

And I think, *That's exactly what you meant*, but I choose not to start a fight in the hotel lobby. 'It's fine,' I say. 'Where to for lunch?'

Mum tells me the restaurant she's booked is a fifteen-minute walk and suggests we get a taxi. She has the man at reception order one, and soon we're on our way. When we arrive, I'm taken aback by the restaurant's humble exterior. 'I think this is the address,' she says, squinting at her phone. 'Yes, it's definitely here.'

Inside, Mum tells me she spent an hour researching which restaurant to bring me to, and I smile, sensing her genuine pride in having discovered this place on her own. 'It's all vegetarian,' she says.

I look up from the menu. 'So I've noticed. That's really cool. Thank you.'

She grins.

The moment is short lived, though, because on her next breath, she says, 'So tell me: what happened with Hugo?'

'I don't know, really.'

She frowns. 'He must have given you a reason.'

'I broke up with him, Mum.'

'What?' she says, not bothering to hide the shock in her voice. '*Why?*'

I shrug. 'I told you: I don't really know.'

'Well, can you take it back?' she asks. 'I'm sure it's not too late.'

'I don't want to take it back, okay?'

'But he was so good for you,' she says, and considering she's never met him, I'm sure she means, *He was safe. He was security.* But there's also a tinge of truth to it. He *was* good for me. He was everything. Like the ocean: open, generous and stretching.

Beautiful. Even as you're drowning in it.

'I just don't understand,' she says.

And I feel myself cast adrift in a sea of memory.

I just don't understand. Over and over.

Talk to me, Oli. Please. Said Hugo. Said Maggie. Said Mac.

And I can't.

Because this colour I see inside me doesn't exist. There's no language for it. No words to describe the shape of this pain. How it glints in the sun. How it overwhelms me so that, suddenly, it's all I can see. Here. There. Everywhere.

Hugo comes into focus now. The marshy borders of memory solidifying so that I'm once more in my apartment, watching his body shudder. Watching him shrink away. Watching his heart rip. And I want to rush to him. To hold him.

But in the blink of an eye, the tide changes and the memory slips back into the deep. His face now watery and without detail. Time disintegrating his words. And into that unanswerable hole, that cavern of blue longing, I feel myself slipping.

'Are you okay?' my mother asks.

I realise tears have welled. 'Yes,' I say, wiping my eyes on the back of my sleeve.

'I'm sorry,' she says. 'Let's talk about something else.'

I nod and she begins talking about my dad. 'He's in America right now. You know him—always off at some conference or another. Always chasing a new business opportunity . . . I keep telling him he needs to retire.' And it strikes me for the first time how little detail she shares about my father's doings. Perhaps it's a sign of how little detail she actually knows.

I ask her what *she's* been doing and she says, 'Oh, you know, I keep myself busy. I've been playing tennis with Abigail. You remember Abigail, don't you?'

'I think so.'

'And Fenella started a book club with another woman, Lily. We're reading a book by Margaret Atwood—have you heard of her?'

I laugh.

'What are you laughing at?'

'Oh, nothing. Yes, I have heard of her. Is it *The Handmaid's Tale*?'

Mum shakes her head. 'No, it's called *Alias Grace*.'

'I think it's great that you're reading.'

Mum chuckles now. 'I'm very slow. But I'm enjoying it.' She takes a sip of her wine.

'If you want, I could give you some recommendations.'

'I would love that,' she says, smiling.

When we've finished lunch, I suggest we walk back to the hotel but Mum, who is wearing heels says, 'Let's just get a taxi.' But after we've waited fifteen minutes, I say, 'Come on, it's not far,' and I set off. Reluctantly, she follows.

We pass boutiques and quaint cafes. A couple strolls by walking a dachshund. We round a corner, and just as I realise where we are I feel a drop of rain land in my hair. Then another. 'Oli . . .' Mum says, but before she has time to finish her sentence, the sky undoes and it begins to pour.

'Quick,' I say, grabbing her hand, 'my gallery is just down the street. Run!'

By the time we reach the gallery, we are soaked. I fumble with the keys, rushing to unlock the door. Opening it, we hurry inside. I flick on the lights and look at my mum. Her hair is sleek and stuck to her face. Mascara is running down her cheeks in black streams. Her lipstick is smudged. She looks like a watercolour left out in the rain.

I'm about to apologise for making her walk when she bursts into laughter, the sound erupting from deep inside of her. And then I'm laughing too. In sprays of pink silver. Wholly and unapologetically. And it feels good. It feels wild and unruly.

Catching her breath, Mum opens her eyes. There's light in them. A timid glow. Faint, but it's there. Unflinching. It's fucking magnificent.

We dry off in the bathroom under the hand dryer, giggling like children. Then we come out into the body of the gallery and I take Mum around to show her our current show. Drawings of clouds drift across the walls, changing shape in each frame.

'You know, I used to draw when I was a girl,' Mum says. 'I loved it. In fact, for a long time, I wanted to be an artist.'

'You've never told me that before.'

'I've never told anyone that before,' she says. And then she adds, 'I think it's amazing what you're doing here,' and I feel the years of distance and desire close up. Right now, in this moment, she's here, with me.

The rain outside has eased. 'Come on,' I say, 'I want to show you something.'

I lock the gallery and we walk down the street to a set of traffic lights. 'Where are we going?' she asks.

The pedestrian light flashes green and we cross the road. 'Here,' I say. We're standing outside an art supply store.

Inside, Mum tells me she couldn't possibly draw now. 'Of course you can,' I say, steering her towards the drawing section, where I pick out a set of pencils and a notepad.

'You should get something too!' she says.

'You're right,' I say, picking up a set of pencils and a notepad for myself.

'We're matching,' she says, and I laugh.

We pay for our purchases and, as we walk out, I see my mother clutching her bag of art supplies to her chest, beaming.

That evening, with Mum on her way to the airport, I take out my notepad and pencils from the brown paper bag. I sit in the middle of the lounge room floor and wonder what to draw. I look outside at the tree beyond the glass, branches without foliage. Naked and gnarled. I begin to draw them, branches twisting at dusk like dark rivers. And though spring is still weeks away, I adorn the tree's arms with pink buds. Ready to bloom.

Hours later, I wake in the thick of the night to my phone vibrating on my bedside table. I look at the screen and see the Australian number. See that I've already missed five calls. I answer.

There is sobbing on the end of the line. He's hysterical. The sound is like nothing I've ever heard in my life.

'What?' I say, frantic. 'Mac? What's wrong?'

But I already know.

red sand

It's like your body takes you in. Takes you somewhere else, somewhere safe, protected; takes you to a place where you feel *nothing*. Nothing of the hurricane. Not the wind. Not the sand like pieces of ice whipped up, whizzing past. Nothing of the fire. Your body takes you in so you can't hear the thunder. So that you're not aware of the tearing, or the ripping. Your body takes you in so that, for a while, you can breathe.

But all storms pass eventually.

And soon I hear the wheels unfurl from the belly of the plane. My ears pop. And then the plane is touching down, bouncing. Gripping. Braking so that I feel myself inching forward in my chair, my belt pulling tight around my abdomen.

All storms pass. And when they do, you crawl out and see that the world is nothing like it was. Fractured walls, torn limbs, broken roofs. The river is dark and muddy, yellow at the edges. Murky water is strewn with leaves and dirt and cracked branches.

I pull my bag down from the overhead compartment, file off the plane with the other passengers and, in the moment I step out of the airport, I don't *see* that the world is not like it was so much as *feel* it. Feel that this wild country of red sand is so big, so overwhelmingly huge, I might cry. It's big where it once felt small, Maggie—like we were the only ones in the room.

I collect my suitcase from the carousel, pass through customs, walk outside.

The earth is big where it once felt small. But the sky: the sky is small where it once felt big. It's low-hanging, pressing down, suffocating me. And in that I feel all the cold, and all the ache.

The taxi drive is long. There's traffic and rain, and soon I feel sick from staring at my phone. I look up and gaze out the window. The droplets on the glass make the buildings outside bleed one into the next.

The air in the taxi smells of steamed fabric and a vanilla freshener. 'Can I wind down my window?' I ask, as I'm already winding it, anxious almost, as if the air in here is no longer real.

'But, Miss, it's raining.'

'I don't mind,' I whisper, closing my eyes, letting the rain pelt my face, letting the years peel away, until at last I'm climbing into the back seat of Mac's car, shaking her hand, touching her for the first time. Listening to her say her name in velvet lilac.

Maggie.

Before I even let go of my bags, Mac's arms are wrapping around me like purple fabric. I shudder and he holds me tighter, and we're suspended in some strange, wonderful, gentle place. Like the world holds its breath, just for a moment. And space is soft.

But then I see Coco emerge from Maggie's bedroom with a chew toy in her mouth. She drops it at the door, comes to my feet, licks my ankle, and I feel myself roll into the blue absence behind her, sinking, unravelling.

Mac puts both hands on my shoulders. His eyes are a swollen lake, dark and full.

'I can't tell you how much we've missed you,' he says.

And I want to tell him how much I've missed them too, how much I've missed *home*, but the words are stuck in my throat.

'She wrote you a letter,' he says. 'Give me a sec.' He disappears into his room, reappearing a few moments later with a folded piece of paper. 'I already know what it says,' he admits. 'I had to write it down for her.'

I look down at the paper in my hands like I'm holding a piece of her.

'I don't know if I'm ready,' I say, shaking my head.

'Don't worry,' he says, and he takes the letter back, places it on the coffee table. 'Another time.'

I sleep in Maggie's bed.

It is everything and nothing. Like a kiss goodbye. Because no matter how tightly I pull the blankets around myself, no matter how tightly I grip the edge of the mattress, I feel adrift in the blue of her.

It's all push and pull. Push and pull. Like she's the tide. Flooding me, and falling away, in a single night. Maggie is all around me. Nowhere.

I inhale. Lungs filling, lungs full. I exhale, and she escapes.

I roll over in bed, eyelids puffy, pick up my phone and see Natasha has forwarded an email from Alison Waite. The subject line jerks me awake. ANTARCTICA.

Has she accepted? Please confirm asap.

I lock the phone and bury it under my pillow. Feeling charged and restless now, I get up and walk out into the kitchen. Unsure what to do with myself, I boil the kettle, put loose-leaf chamomile tea in a glass teapot, pour water over and watch it yellow. I watch flowers soften. I watch petals unfurl. And then with my pot of watery flowers and a mug, I take the letter from the coffee table and go out onto the balcony overhanging the harbour. The water is blue spread out before me, magnificent and bold, like an Yves Klein body.

My dearest Oli,

Perhaps it's comforting to know it's all already here. That everything before and everything that will come after is already here.

Past. Present. Future. Happening all at once.

My dear, everything in the cosmos is connected. In that way, we never really lose each other.

I know it feels like we do. I know you're hurting. Believe me, I know you're hurting. And I know that pain is real. We feel heartache in our bodies, in our bones. Honour that. It's human. It makes us. Makes our stories.

But also believe me when I say that loss is an illusion. Goodbyes are not forever, because everything is already here, becoming, unbecoming, becoming. Just changing form, shape and colour.

A whisper becomes a rib bone, becomes a turn in a river, becomes an embrace, becomes a mountain, un-becomes in a kiss, becomes a spark, becomes a cloud, rains down, becomes a mother, becomes a deep-sea current.

It's all around you, Ol. It's all already here.

We lose people in the form of them that we knew and loved.

But the universe hasn't lost me, I've just become something else.

All my love, in every colour,
Maggie

I hold her in my hands. On my lap. I hold her.

Mac pulls up to a traffic light. The car slows, stops. I feel the weight of her. The absence of her. This tiny box. I wonder at a life reduced, a body burnt down to a box, a tiny box of ashes. Everything she was. All velvet lilac. Everything. Powder and purple smoke.

We lose people in the form of them that we knew and loved.

I hold the box tight against me.

'You alright, kid?'

I nod and a tear slides free. Mac reaches across, carefully wipes it from my cheek.

'I know,' he says. 'Me too.'

When we get out of the car, I pass her to Mac. He walks with her down the dock one last time.

A flock of seagulls takes flight, their shadows flitting across Mac's shoulders like sky dancers. I look up, watch them circle higher, higher still, until they're small, so small, they're like flecks of ash carried away in the wind.

The *Sea Rose* is tied up at the end of the dock. Mac passes me the box and boards her starboard deck, climbing up over the lifeline with the ease of a man twenty years younger. That's what coming home looks like.

I pass the box up to him and he takes her to the cockpit, unhooks the hatch, and disappears downstairs. I look down at my feet, eyeing the thin water corridor between the dock and the hull of the *Sea Rose.* I imagine myself falling through, sandwiched between. The pressure. Pinching darkness. As the world around me bleeds into itself. It's all muddy blue. Deep ocean mud.

But then I hear Mac moving about below deck, below the sea. And I remember she is down there, with him. I feel air rush into me in one sweet deep wash. It's like diving beneath a wave in the thick of the night. I reach up, grip the lifeline, exhale, and cross the water corridor. It's like crossing the horizon from desert to sky.

On deck, my legs are shaky. I steady myself against the mast and close my eyes. Feeling the *Sea Rose* rocking, as if she is my cradle. Soothing me. Sending me to sleep. It is, at once, familiarly strange and strangely familiar. Rocking, back and forth. Back and forth. I breathe. In and out. Back and forth.

That's how it feels coming home.

There's barely enough breeze in the harbour to get us to the heads, but I know Mac: there's no way he'll let the motor drown out the sound of Maggie's last sail. So we drift—for hours, maybe—towards the heads, the occasional gust filling the sails, edging us forward.

When we pass North Head, the wind picks up and the *Sea Rose* lifts. I climb up and sit on the rail, dangling my feet over the side, cutting lines in silk water with my toes. The sea splashes up my calves. A laugh rushes out of me. A crack in the towering cliff face seems to curve into a smile.

I look over my shoulder at Mac. He's at the helm with one hand at the wheel, the other resting on the box beside him.

Beyond him, the Tasman stretches like a bather in the sun. I feel the years falling, back, until I'm standing here in a silk dress, accusing an old man with a white beard of kidnapping me.

'I'm so happy I passed out on your boat,' I tell him.

'You what?' he says.

I laugh, shake my head.

Above, the sail slackens and begins to flap, huge white wings fluttering. Mac reaches down and pulls on the main. And like a seabird, we take flight. His smile stretches the width of the horizon.

We sail through a painting of sounds. No words, just the sun-lanced yellow of waters lapping. The pink of Mac's fingertips pattering the wheel. The smooth blue of the breeze passing between the sails.

We sail through a painting of sounds, all the way to Pittwater, where the Hawkesbury River empties out into the sea. And as the sails drop, I remember a story about streams and deep lakes and meetings at the river mouth. How we all come together in the end.

Mac picks up the box, manages a shaky smile. 'It's time.'

I follow him up to the bow of the boat, where he opens the box. Opens up the clouds. Opens up my chest.

And then I see her. She is sand. Crushed seashells.

I've just become something else.

'Thank you,' Mac says, 'for helping me to see.'

I touch Mac's hands to steady them. Together, we pour her into the sea. And just like that, she becomes part of the ocean, part of my ocean. She becomes a deep-sea current. Seashell bones on the summer tide. Maggie becomes something else.

'I read the letter,' I say.

'I thought you had.'

'How'd you know?'

'Because you're on a boat, and you swore you'd never go to sea again.' Mac taps the seat beside him. 'Come here, kid,' he says, offering me the wheel. I move across the cockpit and sit beside him, taking over at the helm. Mac reaches across me, pulls on the main. I look up and see creases in the sail above ironed out. The boat lifts. I close my eyes, breathe in deep, and feel myself fill with a cloud of salt.

Wrapping his arm around my shoulder, Mac squeezes me tight against his side. 'What you gonna do, then, kid?'

I look south, past Mac's arm, into open ocean, into the beyond.

Becomes a cloud. Rains down. Becomes a mother.

And I think of her telling me how all the souls in the world return to the Antarctic. How we all go home. And I imagine her being carried there on the tide.

'I'm going,' I tell him, myself, her. 'I have to.'

He laughs. The sound is warm tangerine. 'She told me you'd say that.'

sea ice

cloud

'. . . our descent into Ushuaia. We expect to land in approximately twenty minutes. Local time on the ground is nine seventeen am.'

My cheek is cold against the window. I peel open my eyes to see the earth reaching, stretching up through cloud. The plane angles and we glide down into white, emerging above the shoulder of a mountain the colour of thunder, an archaic purple as deep as time itself. Lashes of muddy snow paint its ridges grey. The plane angles again, and we drop down the mountain's steep neck, curve around its shoulder. I touch my palm to the window; the glass is fringed with tiny icicles. I trace the purple body spread out before me with my fingertip.

As we descend, more of it comes into focus, blotches of red earth like freckles. Green trees like pores in the mountain's skin. Breathing, in and out, in and out. My breath clouds the window. I wipe away the white with my sleeve to see the earth unfold into blue. The plane's shadow skims across the water.

The wheels touch the runway. Brakes lock. The pressure eases as we come to a slow roll. I yawn and my ears unblock. I love it when that happens: how you don't realise your attention to the outer quality of the world is less until it is again more. Like heartache, the way it rips you open, exposes you, makes you hypersensitive to the cold, to whispers, to light. I sit back. Maggie's face flashes with the same abruptness as my ears popping and I feel my heart mark itself bright violet against my ribs, the beat suddenly more pronounced.

Outside, as the plane comes to a standstill, the landscape beyond the tarmac takes shape. The first thing I notice are the wildflowers, long stems dotted with pastel pinks, vivid reds, chalk oranges. The second is the grass, green tinged yellow, the coarseness of the tufts, the harshness of it all.

We disembark the plane and as I'm walking across the tarmac, a breath of air sweeps across the runway, grabs me. I shiver, the chill cascading down my spine into my legs.

A woman with silver hair and wide cheeks looks at me and says, 'Feel that?'

I nod, breathe out a plume of white heat. I breathe in. The cold bites my lungs with a rawness I've never felt before.

The woman smiles. 'That's Antarctica.'

Ushuaia, where I'll spend the next few days, is a cluster of brightly coloured houses punctuated by grey concrete. Wildflowers push through cracked pavements. The streets crumble at the edges. Unpainted concrete walls are stained with watermarks. Paint peels. And yet the town feels neither half finished nor like it is falling apart; there is only the sense that it is weathered.

My calves are burning from the walk up through town, the ascent from my hotel down on the waterfront having been steeper than I imagined. I sit on a concrete staircase to catch my breath. A local woman passes me with a child on her back. I manage a smile, still trying to slow my heavy breathing. The woman has barely broken a sweat.

Then she is gone and I am alone here, perched on a staircase above Ushuaia. Beneath me are cars and trucks caked with mud. There's the squeals of children playing in an alleyway, the crowing of roosters. Beyond is the Beagle Channel, today like rippled steel. Beyond that is Isla Navarino, mountains capped with snow that glints yellow in the sunlight. And beyond those brilliant peaks, I know, is the Drake Passage, stretching all the way to Antarctica. In three days' time I'll be pushing out of the Beagle Channel into the blue beyond. Once, land fading from sight felt like home coming into focus. Entering the void. The blue monochrome. But now the blue feels overwhelming. Here. There. Everywhere. In me. Filling my lungs until I'm swollen with water. Ripping open. I feel panic surging through me. My bones feel hot. I can't breathe.

But then a gust of wind steals through the city, rising up the stairs. It seizes me. My sweat cools on my skin. I part my lips. The wind tastes of salt. I breathe in the smells of bird feathers and mud and something else I can't place, something old, something utterly unknown to me.

I imagine that this wind first circled in Antarctica, that it was born out of silence. I imagine how it thickened, changed shape, changed direction. I imagine how it licked the sea, clawed at it, dug up waves from the deep. I imagine how it screamed in the night, shaking sailors' knees.

And as it tears through my hair and up behind me, I find a sense of awe blooming inside my body, a deep and unswerving respect for these coarse grasses, that mother with her child, this purple earth, these people, all these wildflowers.

It's a wild wind. Fierce and bitter and alive. Ushuaia endures. And in that thought, I find solace. For I too, endure.

I spend the afternoon in woods that are unlike any I've ever seen. Spread across the forest floor are fallen trees, the debris so thick in parts, you can't see the earth beneath. Bone white branches lie like a skeleton, like whale bones on a beach, time having eaten away all the flesh and muscle. I think of the wild wind I tasted at the edge of the city, and imagine how it must have devastated these woods, how it would have torn and ripped and splintered.

I pause a moment to consider a tree with a trunk thicker than I've ever seen. I tilt my head back to see it stretching up so high it pushes through the forest canopy, flowering into sky.

Then I hear bone branches crunching and turn to see a young couple hiking the trail behind me.

'*Hola!*' the woman says, beaming in the shadow of the giant tree.

'Sorry,' I say, and then attempt my best Spanish, '*yo hablo inglés*.'

'Ah.' The young man laughs. 'No problem,' he says, switching easily into English.

The woman nods at the tree behind my shoulder. 'Impressive, isn't it?'

'I can't believe how big it is.'

'Several centuries old, I'd say,' the man speculates.

I look up again, whisper, 'Whoa . . .'

'Are you in Patagonia by yourself?'

'Yes.'

The woman extends her hand. 'I'm Luciana, and this is Martin.'

I shake both of their hands. 'Oli.'

'Do you want to walk with us?' Luciana asks.

'Sure. Where are you going?'

Martin shrugs. 'Wherever we want.'

Luciana smiles and kisses him on the cheek.

'Perfect.'

As we walk, Luciana takes Martin's hand in hers, their fingers entwined like tree roots fusing together deep beneath the ground. They're younger than me, but their words twist together as if they've been finishing each other's sentences for decades. Their affection is honest, at once wide open and entangled. There's a knowing. The way that they look at each other. The way they share air, share breath. A wide-open sea, vast and undulating. Dive beneath and it is wildly complex. A seabed of barnacles and abalone shells and fish darting in and out of caves of coral. Perhaps that's what love is. Knowing someone's *beneath*.

Martin asks Luciana something in Spanish.

'Lichen,' she says.

Martin points to a frilled moss sprouting from a tree trunk. 'Lichen,' he says to me. 'It grows where the air is pure.'

I draw air deep into my lungs. Feel frilled green unfold inside me. The air tastes of water-swollen wood and damp earth. Birdsong drifts through the branches.

'Was there a storm?' I ask.

'A storm?' Luciana repeats, puzzled.

'That blew down all these trees,' I explain.

She giggles. Martin shakes his head. 'These trees would have fallen decades ago.'

'The air keeps them,' Luciana says.

'*Keeps?*' I repeat. 'What do you mean?'

'Patagonia is narrow, we have the sea on both sides; the temperature is almost the same the whole year round.'

'It's like a fridge here,' Martin adds.

'Exactly—it stops the wood from breaking down.'

Luciana crouches, touches a fallen trunk, peels back a fleck of bark to reveal the damp green beneath. 'Most are still alive.'

'How?' I ask.

'The trees are all together—' she pats the earth '—underneath.'

Martin elaborates, 'When one tree falls, those around it feed it through their roots.'

And just like that, the earth seems to move, because I imagine the trees, in their embrace, nourishing each other *beneath*. The deepest love.

Luciana smiles. 'The forest: it's one.'

The afternoon before we're due to set sail, Luciana and Martin pick up Joan and me from our hotel in Ushuaia. Joan is a photojournalist from New York who I met at breakfast when she asked me to pass the maple syrup for her mountain of pancakes. She photographed Antarctica ten years ago and is coming back now to document our expedition. She tells me Antarctica will change me. I wonder about that: if a person can be changed by a place; *how* a person can be changed by a place.

Now, sitting in the back of Luciana and Martin's jeep, turning off the highway onto a dirt road, I wonder what kind of person I am to begin with. What kind of person I am *today, yesterday, tomorrow*? I feel the weight of me bouncing in my seat. How do you know? How do you know where you end if you don't know where you start? *Can* you know?

'Wow!' Joan exclaims, angling her camera out the window.

As the jeep rounds a corner, we see the cliff face drop into a valley.

'What's that?' Joan asks, pointing to a strange path winding through the valley. All along its parched edge, bare trunks stick upright like toothpicks. Other trees have fallen, though they're not the same as the trees on the forest floor. These are bleached white, like bone coral; blood sucked dry, littering the banks of a cracked riverbed in the belly of a lush valley.

'Are they old trees too?' I ask.

Martin shakes his head. 'Beavers. They were introduced at the turn of the century and bred for their fur, but when their fur became harsh and scratchy in the new environment, they were set free.'

'The government has been trying to get rid of them for years because they destroy the rivers,' Luciana says, turning down a steep track.

At the bottom, we park on gravel at the edge of a lake. Emerald, smooth and flat like a sheet of glass.

'See over there?' Luciana says, pointing out the window, across the water. 'That's Chile!'

Chile is towering peaks. Purple outlined in striking violet. Wrinkled earth and strange grooves. Eroded troughs, like someone has sunk an elbow into the sides of the mountains.

We get out of the car. Joan snaps a tuft of wildflowers, then points her lens across the lake. She lowers her camera, turns to Luciana and says, 'I've never seen a mountain that shape before.'

'There was a glacier there, once,' Luciana says.

An impression of a body in the *before*.

'The last of it melted a few years ago,' Martin says.

'We've lost ten in the last thirty years.' Luciana locks the jeep. 'There are only three we can still hike to.'

'And they're all retreating too.'

I look back to Joan. There are tears in her eyes. 'Imagine if these glaciers were paintings in the Louvre,' she says, 'just melting off the walls. People don't realise *this* is our history too.'

The path we walk from the lake to the Beagle Channel cuts through dense forest. As we walk, Luciana tells me about the beech trees in Patagonia, how it's the small ones that lose their foliage, peppering the forest floor with opal-shaped leaves. There is a leaf in every shade of orange. In fact, though the clouds hanging above are thick grey, I've never walked through such vivid colour. Yellow mosses are fringed with purple. There are orchards in green, blue and white. Black roots and red soil. An Impressionist painting.

'This mushroom, at the right time, tastes like a peach,' Luciana says. 'The Yamana call it *sweet sweet*.'

'Who are the Yamana?' I ask.

'The First Nations Peoples of this area,' she replies.

'The southernmost people in the world,' Martin adds.

'In their tongue, *Yamana* means *human*.'

'Theirs is an incredibly succinct language,' explains Martin. 'They have a word meaning *cold in your whole body*.'

'And another word,' says Luciana, 'to describe a look between two people, where each of them expects the other to start something, but neither does, because they're both waiting on the other to begin first.'

I see Hugo's eyes, dense black. Sinking into me. I know that look. The blue of desire and longing. The blue of unspoken words. I steady myself against a tree. Feeling the wetness in the bark.

'Are you okay?' Martin asks.

I nod. 'Just a little light-headed.'

'We'll be at the beach soon. We can sit there and have something to eat.'

Luciana takes my hand. Her skin is cool like water. We begin walking, still holding hands. I close my eyes a moment, letting her guide me, and listen to the colours of the forest, to the yellow of a cabbage daisy squashed beneath a boot, to the mauve creaks of branches overhead.

I open my eyes, and Luciana tells me about winter's bark, how the Yamana chewed it for its vitamins and used the leaves to brew spicy tea. How they peppered sea lion with its seeds.

We emerge onto a beach of smooth stones. Large rocks at the water's edge are encrusted with mussels. We sit among wildflowers and wisps of grass. Martin hands out cheese sandwiches.

Behind us, the earth is uneven mounds beneath grass, like a green sheet laid over sleeping bodies. Martin tells us that if you dug down into the mounds, you'd dig through thousands of years of history. 'Fish bones, mussels, clothing . . .' he says, explaining how the Yamana would heap their leftovers in piles that then built up over the centuries.

I touch my hand to the earth and imagine the stories buried beneath.

'The Yamana were a water people, weren't they?' Joan says.

'Yes,' says Luciana, 'they hunted on the channel in canoes, lighting fires in the boats to keep warm while they caught sea lions in nets made of kelp.'

'What happened to them?' I say, though, knowing the truth of the dead trees in the valleys, there is a weight deep inside me, a sad knowing before Luciana even answers.

'Some have survived, but many were wiped out by the Europeans,' she says, gazing out across the channel.

I think of Joan's comment about the Louvre. *This is our history too.*

'I often try to imagine myself here a thousand years ago,' Martin says.

I close my eyes, imagining forests of kelp and sea bugs, spiders and crabs.

'It makes me sad,' Luciana says, 'to know how much is missing.'

'Yeah,' I say. 'And scared for the future.'

Martin finishes his sandwich and goes over to a nearby bush, picking off a handful of berries. He passes one to me. 'There is a saying that if you eat one of these berries, you have to come back to the island.'

I take one and pop it in my mouth. It's as sweet as it is sour.

At the end of the trail, there is a lonesome post office, with a sign reading *the last post office at the end of the world.* I buy a postcard and write:

Dear Mac,

You wouldn't believe the colours I've seen.

Tomorrow, Antarctica!

All my love,

Oli

snow

The gangway onto the *Sea Spirit* is wobbly. Or I am wobbly. Or both.

A member of the crew who is welcoming people aboard notices my hesitancy. 'First time at sea?'

'Um . . .'

'Don't worry,' she says. 'You'll have your sea legs in no time!'

'Hopefully,' I say, and step aboard, feeling the ship lurch beneath me. The movement, back and forth, is tender. Both gentle and painful.

I'm shown to my cabin. Its walls are made of dark wood with smooth varnish. I flop back onto the bed as an announcement comes on over the speaker calling all passengers into the main cabin for a safety briefing.

In the main cabin, everyone takes a seat in armchairs that are bolted to the floor. This ship is made for *big* waves.

The woman who welcomed me aboard walks up to the front of the room and introduces herself as Salma, the expedition leader. She's tall with broad shoulders and long black hair. There is something about her that makes me feel safe; it's not her size, but the way she speaks about the Drake Passage. She has an acute awareness of the ocean's unknowability that instantly reminds me of Mac.

As she runs through the weather forecast, a woman sits down in the chair beside me, whispering an apology to Salma for her tardiness.

Salma smiles and introduces the latecomer. 'Everybody, this is Brooke, she's our resident glaciologist.' She then goes on to introduce the rest of the crew.

After the initial briefing is over, members of the crew hand out life jackets.

Brooke turns to me. 'Have we met?'

'No,' I say. 'I don't think so.'

'You look wildly familiar. Are you famous?'

'Not at all,' I say, laughing. And then she laughs too, and with the curve of her smile, a scar appears. It stretches from the edge of her lip to the corner of her eye. I tilt my head and ask, 'Are *you*?', because in the crease of skin, in the depth of her laugh, I too find something familiar.

Brooke shakes her head. 'Sometimes, we just know, right?'

I think of Maggie. How meeting her felt more like a returning. Two rivers meeting, flowing from the same spring.

I extend my hand. 'My name's Oli.'

Brooke doesn't shake my hand. She leans across and hugs me. And I have this strange feeling that we've been here before.

When the briefing is over, Brooke invites me to the bar for a drink.

'Sorry,' I say, 'I'm exhausted.' I'm playing nervously with a ring on my finger. My hands are shaking.

Perhaps she notices, because she asks, 'Have you been at sea before?'

'Not for a while.'

'You anxious?'

'Just worried I'll get seasick,' I lie, and I think she can tell, but she doesn't push me further.

'Rest up,' she says.

I smile. 'Yeah, see you round.'

From the porthole in my cabin, I watch rigid mountain peaks soften into smooth, sloping hills, the earth unravelling into the sea, until land is a mere smudge on the horizon. And the sea is all around me. Opening out. Closing in.

I climb into bed, my legs trembling. Dinner is called, but I can't move.

I pull the blankets up to my neck and squeeze my eyes shut, but all I see is ocean. And it's suffocating. Because the weight of the sea is oppressive. I feel it everywhere, like I'm on the ocean floor. In ocean mud. Wrapped in coils of seaweed. Tied up. Blue-bound. Buried in an underwater cemetery. My cries silenced by a water so vast I feel it will take centuries for my words to reach the surface.

I roll over and turn on my bedside lamp. Finding my purse, I pull out the sleeping pills my doctor prescribed for the plane. I go to the bathroom, fill a glass and swallow the pill with a mouthful of water. Shuffling back across the room, I get into bed and lie down on my back. Staring at the ceiling, I wait for the pill to draw my eyelids down. For it all to empty out.

Hours later, I wake with beads of sweat strung around me like a necklace of pearls. I sit upright and wipe the sweat from between my breasts with my nightshirt. It's awfully hot in here. I need air. Real air. Night air.

I switch on the lamp and get up, pulling on my thermal stockings and snow pants, my thermal top, fleece and down jacket. I put on my gloves, snow socks, beanie and hiking boots. Lastly, I wrap a scarf around my neck.

I'm burning up.

He was in my dream.

Four years later, and he was in my dream with the pungency of fish guts raining down from the heavens.

He was in my dream the way he was in me. Unbearably. Then, now, forever? Cum dripping down my thighs.

He pulled out, but he never left. That's what it is. That's what kills us. It's the incessant lingering, the hanging on, so that in still and silent moments, I feel him. When I'm stopped at a traffic light. Or in the pause before the shower turns on, waiting to feel something *else*. I feel him inside me, still there, spreading himself, spreading himself wide red, making himself big. And there's an expanding inside me, an expanding like a pipe is pumping air into my lungs so that they fill with someone else's breath, filling, filling, my ribs pulling apart. Skin stretching. Skin tearing. Blood and cum. Someone else's breath in me, breathing for me. I can't breathe. *I can't breathe.*

I scramble up the stairs to the upper deck, push through the door, burst out into darkness.

We choose to breathe, don't we?

I stumble, roll my ankle, trip, hit the deck with a slam that echoes through bone, a slam that makes me feel alive. I clamber to my feet, grip the handrail; drag myself along the starboard deck to the bow of the ship. I seize the railing with both hands as the boat sails over a peak in the swell, surfs down the back of it, smashes into the oncoming wave, sending sea spray flying like a flock of silver birds in a frenzy. The sky is pressing down, leaning in on me. The ship lifts on another wave, and the sky seems so close I think I might puncture it, burst through the skin of the night, disappear into the beyond.

The ship shivers. Surfs down. Slams into him. He's here. He's always here. He stalks me. Still. In the sanctuary of dreaming. He stalks me.

I cling to the rail, blood pulsing, my knuckles white. The night is wet velvet. I inhale. The air cuts my lungs, slices open flesh.

The boat lifts, surfs down, slams. My body is thrust against the rail, and out of me, in the darkness, comes something animal, something feral. I scream.

I scream not in the way the damsel in distress screams from the tower. I scream the way tectonic plates tear apart on the ocean floor, silt and sand and cracked rock. Lava spewing from the abyss. Hot lava spewing from me. I roar.

Feel myself split open. Flesh cleaved apart. Silt and sand and cracked rock. Lava bubbles up. *He* bubbles up. I ROAR. The sound rips open my throat. He's scratching, clawing, still holding on.

And I realise. Here I am. I've been here. Tied up, blue-bound, for years. On the ocean floor. In ocean mud. But now, the ocean floor is moving. Lava pours. It courses through cold purple caves, spreads, I am all spreading. I am moving. I am rising.

I scream, 'HERE I AM. I AM HERE!' And in that instant, I feel him explode through the surface. Hot red sprays across black night.

'HEAR ME!' I scream. 'HEAR ME NOW!'

Tears are pouring hot pink. Here I am. I am alive. I am open. I am here. I wipe my eyes on the back of my sleeve. Here I am. I survived. I survived!

I breathe in and the night sky fills me up with seashells and salt.

Sick yellow flowers into stars. Here I am. I choose to breathe.

glacier

I run into Brooke on the staircase on my way to breakfast.

'Good morning,' I say.

'Great morning,' she replies, and I laugh.

Brooke looks at me quizzically. 'You look different.'

'In what way?' I ask.

'Like you've got your sea legs back.'

My smile pinches my cheeks. 'Yeah. I guess I have.'

She pats me on the back. 'Come on,' she says. 'I'm hungry.'

Two of the artists I exhibited at *WOMXN* in London, Holly and Vivienne, are on the expedition. We find them at the breakfast bar and I introduce them both to Brooke. Then we all join Joan at a table.

Over breakfast, we talk about where Holly and Vivienne have been since the show. Holly has been in New York, Vivienne in Paris.

'I never thanked you properly,' says Vivienne. 'After the show, people started to take my work a lot more seriously.'

I feel myself swelling with pride. 'So they should,' I say.

'I still struggle to get people to take my work seriously,' Brooke says, laughing. 'Especially men. Especially men I'm dating.'

'Ha!' says Joan. 'I know the feeling.'

'They're probably intimidated,' Holly tells her.

'With me it's the opposite,' says Brooke. 'They all try to make me smaller. One guy I went out with referred to my DPhil at Oxford as my "little project". Another used to say I worked with "ice and stuff".'

Holly says, 'My last boyfriend asked when I was going to get a real job!'

And we all crack up.

'Well,' says Brooke, 'I realised down here, standing at the foot of a glacier bigger than they could ever imagine, that I'm a fucking superstar.'

'Hear, hear!' says Joan, raising her glass of orange juice.

'And you know what?' says Brooke. 'I fucking love my life. I don't need to be with someone unless they add to it.' Her smile is wider than the sky. 'I'm not afraid of the risk of being woman.'

And to that, we all clink glasses.

Later, those of us not affected by seasickness gather in the main cabin for games of cards. We play Shithead and I laugh until my sides are sore. But it feels good, this ache. Because it's born out of something unashamedly honest. And I don't care that I suck at this game, because I feel like I've won, either way.

At lunch, Salma announces that we're halfway to Antarctica, but adds that a growing swell is likely to slow us down.

'The Southern Ocean,' she says, 'is a great place to learn patience.'

When we wake on our third day, the swells that peaked overnight are slowly dying. The boat is steadying. Salma gathers everyone in the main cabin for the morning's announcements. She tells us we're nearing the peninsula and says there'll be a prize for the first person to spot an iceberg.

'Congratulations, everyone, for surviving the Drake Passage!' she says and we all cheer loudly.

At breakfast, I learn that one of the chefs, Alex, is Australian and has a tub of Vegemite in the kitchen. I spread it over my toast for the first time in years, grinning like a child.

Brooke finds me making a coffee. 'It's safe to go outside,' she says. 'The swell's dropped off enough.'

'Should we eat brekkie on deck?'

'You read my mind.'

I fold my toast up in a napkin and take my coffee back to my room, where I rug up. I haven't been outside since we entered the Drake Passage, and now that we're much further south the air is shocking. It's a cold that completely consumes. Like falling in love. Total and unapologetic.

Brooke meets me on deck, and we walk together up to the bow.

'Hey!' someone calls out.

We look up to the bridge to see a woman in uniform waving.

'Who's that?' I ask Brooke.

'That's our captain, Georgia—she's a weapon,' Brooke says, and I laugh.

A moment later, an albatross appears above the starboard deck. I tap Brooke on the shoulder, 'Look! Look!'

'Beautiful, isn't she?' Brooke says as the bird soars across the bow of the boat in front of us, wings stretched out wide, a smooth shadow flying over the deck. 'She's young,' Brooke says. 'She'll grow to be twice that size.'

'Incredible,' I whisper, thinking of Mac. And then. Of Maggie and Coco. Of another sea in another time. Flashing before me. Flooding back. A memory so palpable, I feel I could reach out and touch them. Hold their hands.

I think of Robynne. Home, here, in Antarctica. And I can hear myself asking Mac, all those years ago, on the *Sea Rose*, 'Do you ever wonder what the point was?'

'The point,' he'd told me, 'was that she lived.'

Brooke grabs my arm, and I'm drawn back into the present. 'Oli!' she says. 'Look! Over there!'

Looking in the direction in which she is pointing, I see it. Our first iceberg. A bold white block on the horizon. We run into the main cabin to let the others know.

Salma is by the stairs.

'Iceberg!' I shout. 'Iceberg!'

Brooke laughs. 'Don't shout *that*! Haven't you seen *Titanic*?'

Our first landing is at Half Moon Island, a crescent-shaped sliver of rock.

Before we disembark the ship, we have to vacuum all our clothing to remove any trace of flora from South America, and wash our expedition boots in a quarantined room. I'm wearing so many layers, I seem to waddle, not walk. 'Like a penguin,' says Brooke.

We climb down off the stern deck into inflatable boats called zodiacs. In my boat are Salma, Brooke, Vivienne, Holly, Joan and Alice, a sculptor and textiles artist from Australia. She has a head of thick red hair that makes me think I'm among Vikings. Fearless women, braving the sea at the end of the earth.

When we land on the beach, Brooke points out an old wooden boat, shipwrecked at the end of the island.

I imagine the men who landed here more than a hundred years ago. Ghosts climbing out of the boat. Footsteps on the moon, this cragged half.

Brooke helps me out of the boat. Waves lapping at the shore, like gentle kisses in the middle of the night. Smooth pebbles, rounded and softened by this intimacy.

'A *real* penguin!' Brooke says, pointing to a cluster of penguins up on the ridge above the beach. 'They're chinstrap penguins. Look at their faces—it's like they're wearing hats with little straps around their chins.'

Vivienne climbs out next, holding her camera high to save it from being splashed by a wave. 'Oh my God,' she says. 'They're adorable!'

I help the others out, then we push the zodiac off the beach so Salma can return to the ship for another group.

The sky is wide open. Clear as crystal. I remember how, at dinner, Salma had said, 'Antarctica is the lungs of the planet.' I breathe into it. Into the sky. Feel the entire world flowing through me.

We wander to the end of the island, where a huge cliff face juts out vertically from the earth. Rounding it, I gaze up, feel a wave of awe wash over me. The cliff face is blackened, as if charred, with tendrils of orange lichen rising up like tongues of fire. Around its base, sea lions lounge, blending in so well with the landscape that Vivienne almost walks into one. It rears its head, eyeing her. She takes a step back, saying, 'Sorry, hon. You do you . . .' and the rest of us burst into laughter.

Back on the pebbly beach, I notice, all along the shoreline, are strange jelly-like creatures, each dotted with a blood red spot. 'What are they?' I ask Brooke.

'They usually live in the waters around South America, but because the water is getting warmer here, they're all coming south.'

Holly asks, 'Is that a bad thing?'

'Yeah,' says Brooke, crouching down for a closer inspection. 'They eat the same plankton as the krill. Which means that, for the first time, the krill are having to compete for their food source.'

'So there'll be less krill?'

Brooke nods. 'Exactly—and *everything* here relies on krill.'

Overnight, we sail from the South Shetlands archipelago down to the Antarctic Peninsula. I wake to Salma's voice over the loud-speaker giving the weather report and mapping out the day's activities, starting with kayaking after breakfast. There's a knock at my door.

I open it to find Brooke.

'Be my kayak buddy?' she asks, grinning.

'Ha! Of course!' I say, and she high fives me.

'Now get your clothes on, quick—Georgia just said they saw orcas from the bridge.'

'Orcas!' I exclaim. 'Like killer whales?'

'Yes,' says Brooke, laughing. 'Same thing.'

I rush back into my room and start getting ready. Brooke comes in and flops down on my bed. 'Wear thermals and leggings to go under your kayak dry suit,' she says.

'Are these okay?'

She nods and I wriggle into my thermals, pull a jumper over my head, chuck on my jacket, and the two of us are out the door, running like children through the ship to the port deck. 'Over there!' squeals Brooke.

I follow her gaze to a pod of orcas, poking their heads between sheets of ice. The sky's warming into pink. And even though the sun is rising, the moon is still visible above the ice. And I remember a picture I saw in a book once, in a room where root tentacles spread in water flowerbeds. A book about whales. How I'd described this exact scene to a woman who saw my voice in strokes of red. And there's the feeling that time is catching up. Or maybe I am falling back. Back through the pages. Through paper-thin years. To her.

Brooke holds my hand, and I realise I am crying.

'You okay?'

'Yeah,' I say with a wet smile. 'I just saw an old friend.'

After breakfast, we anchor in a bay sheltered from the wind. Brooke and I are first into the kayaks. Lowered in, we begin to paddle. And as the sea turns to glass, we find ourselves paddling on sky, blue mountains rippling beneath us.

I look over my shoulder and say to Brooke, 'Do you ever get the feeling that this place is strangely familiar?'

'Absolutely,' she says.

'Yeah . . . Why is that?'

Brooke shrugs. 'I never knew my birth mum. Not until I was twenty-five and meeting her for the first time. But when I did meet her, I was in a park I'd never been to, in a state I'd never been to, meeting a woman whose name I didn't know. Yet it was strangely familiar. Like my body remembered her body.'

I turn from Brooke, look out at Antarctica stretching before us. A body. Androgynous. Blanketed by a glacier. A frozen river, flowing from the sky into the sea.

'Antarctica is like that,' she says. 'The body remembers . . . Like, when you look into the ice, you see where you came from. It's so distant, you don't recognise it consciously, but your body does. Your body remembers where it came from.'

A piece of ice bobs in the water beside the kayak. 'That's glacier ice,' says Brooke. 'It's clear because all the air has been squeezed out of it over millions of years. Those glaciers—' she points up ahead '—they take thousands of years to flow down mountains. The distance you or I could walk in five seconds could take a glacier fifty thousand years to travel.'

I feel the air rush out of me, feel the pause between heartbeats.

I look at my watch. It's stopped working in the cold.

Brooke smiles. 'You're on planet time now.' Then she passes me her paddle and says, 'Hold this, will you?'

She leans over and fishes out the chunk of glacier ice and puts it on her lap.

'Are we allowed to do that?' I ask.

'It's going to melt anyway,' she says. 'And besides, it will be perfect for our Baileys on ice tonight.'

'You're a genius,' I say.

Brooke grins.

The others have caught up to us now. Joan and Alice in one kayak, Vivienne and Holly in another. Behind them, more women, laughing and chatting.

'Okay, everyone,' says Cath, the kayak leader, raising her paddle into the air. 'We're all going to be quiet now and listen to the glacier.'

We lift our paddles from the water and rest them across our laps, all breathing quietly now.

In the distance, there are cracks and groans. The ice rubs, caresses, pushes, pulls. Like making love. How two bodies fold together. How I held hands once with Hugo. And there's a feeling of history happening all at once. Because when I peer over the edge of the kayak into the tide, I realise that this body of water stretches. From here it flows through oceanic pits and tropical reefs. Around capes and towering cliffs. Across deep channels and shallow bays. Up the river, winding through the earth. To Hugo. Where I imagine him, standing, right now, on the banks of the Thames, peering over the railing, into the same body of water. Our reflections rippling into each other. The faraway nearby.

'Thank you,' I whisper into the tide. 'For everything.' And I know my words, carried through this ancient sea in wide undulations, reach him. In another time, he hears me.

iceberg

We climb down into the zodiac for our landing at Neko Harbour and Salma runs us ashore. On the way, between the ship and the beach, we pass an iceberg as tall as a twenty-storey building. 'Wow!' exclaims Vivienne. 'Can we go any closer?'

Salma shakes her head. 'Sorry. What you're seeing is probably one-tenth of what's beneath the surface. If I go any closer, I'd risk hitting it underwater.'

The iceberg is the most impressive sculpture I've ever seen. And as it dawns on me that one day this will melt and become a part of the sea, I realise that loss and beauty are bound together inextricably.

'Icebergs wear their stories on their skin,' says Salma. 'Those ridges on its side would tell us when that side was underwater, maybe even for how long.'

Brooke pokes me. 'And that's only what's above the surface. Imagine what other stories lie beneath!'

I hold her hand, imagining that we too are icebergs. All of us. Women. Rising to the surface. That is what you see us by. But beneath the surface, we are spreading. We are powerfully demanding of space.

Neko Harbour is a gentle curve from a headland covered with penguins to a mountain that stands so tall it blocks out the sun and dwarfs our ship.

I walk up to the ridge above the beach, turn and look out over the ancient ice. Brooke comes running up beside me. 'Doesn't that make you feel big?' she says, beaming.

'*Big?*'

'Yeah, big. I feel huge!' she says. 'I come down here with men all the time, and they always tell me how they feel reduced here. I think it rattles them, this place. Broadly speaking, they have an urge to conquer, maybe stick their dick in it.'

I crack up.

'I'm serious!' Brooke says. 'Because they're so used to being the big thing. And we've spent our whole lives being small. Oli—' she is standing behind me now, grabbing my arms and stretching them out wide like wings '—*this* is your chance to expand!'

I feel my chest open. I stand on my tiptoes. Stretch out my fingers. I become huge.

'Beware,' Brooke whispers in my ear, 'for I am fearless, and therefore powerful.'

'Beware,' I repeat, shouting it, 'for I am fearless, and therefore powerful!'

Cath and the others are at the edge of the glacier. They hear me shouting, and look up.

'Fuck yeah, you are!' Cath yells.

Together, Brooke and I sing out: *'Beware! For I am fearless! And therefore powerful!'*

We collapse back into the snow, both laughing hysterically. The weight in me, shedding like skin.

That night, a bunch of us plan to sleep on the continent. Not in tents, but in sleeping bags. We land on a rocky beach fringed by compacted snow, and hike up to a plateau above the beach.

In fading light, we dig our beds with shovels, then lay camping mats and our waterproof sleeping bags in them.

The cloud cover is thick, so as the light fades, the sky becomes a black vault. Inky darkness. All around us.

We wriggle into our sleeping bags.

Slowly, the earth becomes still. Until silence is so thick, so palpable, and so real, I could reach out and cut it.

I remember a night sleeping on deck, in the iris of the sea.

Silence, which I had imagined to be beautiful and romantic, is strangely terrifying.

And then, in the early hours of the morning, I'm woken by a clap of thunder that ricochets through the bay. A glacier. The vocal organ of the mountain is beginning to calve. It cracks and folds in on itself, explodes and grinds. I sit up in my sleeping bag.

Across the water, chunks of ancient ice break off, dissolve into the sea. It's heavenly disastrous. This scream. As world stories, embedded in the ice, fall into the grey. Become part of something else. Stories swirling together in a great pool. Returning home. Into the darkness from which we all came. The darkness that we will all return to.

Between. The sea is teal glass. Broken in the middle by a humpback whale, surfacing to breathe.

I smile. 'Morning, Maggie. I knew you'd find me here.'

At dinner, Holly, sitting next to me, asks if I'm still dating that guy I introduced her to at the exhibition opening in London.

I feel myself contract, shrinking away. I shake my head. 'We broke up,' I say. 'Two months ago.'

'Oh, I'm sorry,' she says. 'Are you okay?'

'Yeah. I am. I think.'

She reaches across and finds my hand, holding it tight.

'He was perfect,' I say, 'but that didn't make it right.'

She squeezes my hand and says, 'Well, we're all here for you.'

'Thank you,' I say. 'I guess there were things I needed to figure out. And I felt like I needed to be alone to do it.'

Brooke, on my other side, takes my free hand. 'Leaving someone you love is painful,' she says. 'You're very brave.'

All around the table, the women link hands. And I feel a current circulating. Like a tide. Pulsing. An ocean made up of many moving parts. Pushing and pulling, beneath the surface of one skin.

'It's the deepest red,' I mumble to myself.

Brooke looks at me quizzically. 'What did you say?'

'Deep red . . . it's the deepest red.'

Holly squeezes my hand. 'What is, Oli? What's red?'

'Rape,' I say. The word lands heavy on the table. Out of me. 'I was raped at sea.' Letting go of this secret, I feel faint. Floating in the faraway nearby. 'I've never told anyone that before.'

And I wait for words to puncture skin. But these women say nothing. They just hold my truth.

We stay like this. Hand in hand, for all kinds of stories. Each one breaking off a body and dissolving into the pool between us, like ice calving off a cliff face. One woman talks about her marriage, how it survived the death of a child. Another woman describes raising her daughter alone, how once they'd had nothing but now her daughter's studying for a PhD in physics. Another woman shares a harrowing story about leaving her abusive partner. And we hold hands a little tighter. Another woman tells us how she's just gone into remission.

And I realise, it's not just me. All of our bodies are scarred. But a scar is the way the body becomes whole again. It's evidence that we survived.

'A man did this to me,' Brooke says, smiling so that we can see the scar stretching from her lip to the corner of her eye.

'And you know what's funny?' she says. 'It's how often women say to me, *Don't worry, you're still beautiful*, as if that's what I'm aiming for. You know, the whole "It doesn't matter what you look like, you are beautiful" thing . . .' Brooke laughs. 'I mean, what the fuck? Who cares! Why do I even have to think of that? I want someone to tell me I'm a weapon, or that I'm fun, or challenging, or hilarious. Why is beautiful a thing? Why is it *the* thing? Beautiful for who? Tell me I'm a heroine. Tell me I'm inventive. Actually, tell me I'm a fucking hurricane. Yeah, that's what I want to be—a hurricane.'

She breathes in deep, blows a lungful of air into the circle. And then breathes in deep again, only this time we all join. Inhaling together. Exhaling as one. In a single gust of wind. Magnificent. Triumphant.

We choose to breathe, don't we?

We have Baileys on glacier ice for dessert, clinking glasses with each other at the bar. Yassmin, the poet on board, steps onto the table at the front of the bar, Brooke beside her ringing a bell on the counter to silence everyone.

Yassmin unfolds a piece of paper, clears her throat, and begins to read. 'A poem for Edgar Allan Poe. He wrote: *the death of a beautiful woman is, unquestionably, the most poetical topic in the world.*'

There are murmurs around the room.

'Well,' Yassmin says, 'to that, I say this: *Basalt curl. And Black pearl. Silky Yellow Oyster Shell. "The death of a beautiful woman . . ." Her basalt curl. Her black pearl. Is "unquestionably, the most poetical topic in the world."'*

Yassmin shakes her head, her entire body.

'*Becoming earth. A coffin laced with vines. Blue poppy embroidery. "Bereaved lips," are best to write. The Lovely strings. Of her blue kites . . .* Unquestionably? How I beg to differ. How I beg to disagree. You are so *wrong, Edgar. You are wrong indeed.*'

There are cheers from the audience. Yassmin raises her voice. It's full-bodied. So powerful it gives me goosebumps.

'*For becoming earth is not* HER *Poem. Becoming Earth. Is. Just. One verse.*'

Someone shouts, 'Hear, hear!'

'*A woman is a constellation. More words than you could Ever dream. She is basalt curl and black pearl. Smooth pink oyster shell. Dark red tides and star anise. Infinitely deep is this Chalice. Woman is waxing. She is waning. Two lips touching. Arc of spine and curve of thigh. Author. Poet. Artist. The* only *one to pen the flight. Of her blue kite.*' She takes a deep breath, stamps her foot down on the table. 'So!' she shouts. '*Edgar Poe, I have to say. When you assert the beauty of her death. You miss the sublimity of her every breath. How sad for you. For you miss to see. How ocean exhales cloud. A pink river in the sky.*'

Yassmin raises her arms up and receives a standing ovation. I cheer with all of me.

I'm lying on my bed facing the window when we pass through the narrow water corridor into the heart of Deception Island, a strip of land shaped like a horseshoe. Volcanic black.

In the quarantine room, I find Brooke and the others changing into their expedition boots. I pull on mine, do up the laces.

'Ready?' says Brooke.

I tuck my scarf into my parka. 'Ready!'

We load into the zodiac and motor to shore across water like green silk. There's a glacier bordering the beach. A wall of marbled black and white. Volcanic ash layered among the ancient ice. A story woven in time.

When we climb ashore, a thick fog has descended on the island. The soil is dense black. Like Hugo's eyes. Like AJ's hair. I shudder.

Heading away from the group, I round the bottom of the glacier and walk out onto a ridge, far enough away now that the others' voices are muffled, as if I'm under water, until I'm so deep I can't hear anyone at all.

There is a pulsing. Like waves lapping against the shore. I follow the sound, walking, wandering. Until I realise the sound is within me. Blood pulsing in my temples.

A voice whispers, *Come lay down on my shadow.* I sit down, lie back on the blackened earth. In the shadow of everything before. Feel the weight of my body sinking into itself. I take a deep breath. Feel the sky rush down into me. And I'm okay. I'm here. I take off my gloves. Dig them into the earth. It's warm beneath the surface. Like ash retaining heat long after the fire has gone out. I retain heat.

You set me on fire, I think. *And I survived.*

Brooke climbs up onto the ridge and lies down beside me. She closes her eyes.

'Brooke?' I whisper.

She opens one eye. 'Yeah?'

'This place is so strange. But I feel so at home here.'

She smiles. 'Deserts and ice aren't foreign to women. We've been here for millennia.'

I think of Maggie. Wild violets in the tundra.

Brooke takes a deep breath. 'Okay,' she says, sitting up and grabbing my hand. 'Come on . . . we're all going to jump off the boat.'

'Into the *water*?'

'Yep!'

'In *what*?'

'Your birthday suit?' She laughs. 'After all, it is your birthday tomorrow . . .'

'You're insane,' I say.

'Trust me,' she says, helping me to my feet. 'The water will change you, Oli. Into something else.'

dark pink sea

I shiver, look across the deck, and spy Brooke. She grins and her scar becomes a sun wrinkle. Two sides fold into each other, a warm crease, a wondrous line that stretches from pink lip to blue eye. She winks. I smile and it hurts my face.

One final exhale. One final inhale. Filling, full.

And I dive in.

Beneath, icebergs suspended in the grey, I open my eyes. Darkness is endless, all stretching. There's whale song. The song starts, or stops.

It's a melody, ocean screaming. My melody waxes and wanes. This story ends here. Dark salt. Black pearl. We choose to breathe, don't we?

We choose to breathe, I think. And suddenly it's all dark salt, a neck of black pearls. This story begins here, at the end of the earth. Here, where silence is thick like muscle, a body ancient and strong. And then it fractures, a cliff face cracking, breaking off, dissolving into the sea. The edge of Antarctica, the outer skin, sheds, and frozen stories embedded in its pores thaw and become part of the beyond.

And now I'm under. I'm with her, with you. And the cloud of breath held in my lungs is dark pink, a work of art. My body is cut crystal, glacier ice, refracting. Dying out. Choices memories dreams aches eyes smiling hands touching laughing beating tears. Punctuation is in all the wrong places.

Hear me scream.

I'm a queen tide, full and round, swelling, overflowing. I'm a flood. I am strong. I'm huge. I'm an ice cliff cracking. I'm breaking off. I'm dissolving into the sea. And all the stories in me become part of the beyond.

I just breathed you in.

acknowledgements

I would first like to acknowledge the Traditional Owners of the lands and waters on which I researched this book. I acknowledge the Traditional Owners of country throughout Australia, and recognise their continuing connection to land, waters and culture. I pay my respects to their Elders past, present and emerging.

I discovered Oli at sea. And over time, with the help of many teachers, I learnt a language with which to tell her story.

Thank you to my dad, Will Hardcastle, for teaching me to read the wind on open ocean before I could read words. Thank you to my mum, Lindy Hardcastle, for teaching me to endure storms at sea. Thank you to my nan, Maggie Hardcastle, for reading everything I've ever written . . . I wish you could have read this.

Thank you to Alison and Dave Molloy at Prosail in the Whitsundays for first introducing me to the Coral Sea. Thank you to Peter Lowndes and Sarah Goddard-Jones of Wine Dark

Sea for letting me sail the east coast of Australia with you. I remember so clearly the moment we first listened to whale song together in a garden of sea flowers. Oli would not have met Mac and Maggie if it weren't for you two.

Thank you to everyone at Chimu Adventures for taking me to the end of the earth. Thanks also to Samuel Johnson whose belief in me as an artist helped me to get there. Thank you to everyone who joined me on my adventures through Patagonia and Antarctica. Special thanks go to Gwenllian Bateman and Alicia-Rae Olafsson who shared Antarctica's silences with me.

I discovered Oli at sea, but I wrote her story while studying as a Provost's Scholar at Worcester College at the University of Oxford. The generosity of my scholarship's donors afforded me this immense privilege. Words can't express how grateful I am for this opportunity.

At Oxford, I found a language with which to tell Oli's story by studying under Dr Daniel Matore, Dr Henry Mead and Professor Sir Jonathan Bate. When I wrote *Below Deck*, I read the entire novel aloud to Professor Sir Jonathan Bate. Thank you for listening with such care and open generosity. Thank you for holding my truth.

Thank you also to the great womxn throughout history whose fearless storytelling and fierce activism laid the groundwork that made writing this story possible. Thank you to my literary heroes, Rebecca Solnit, Marianne Moore, Mina Loy and H.D., whose work was especially influential in the creation of *Below Deck*.

Thank you to Professor Elleke Boehmer at the University of Oxford who took me on as her research assistant in 2019, giving me the opportunity to further research Antarctic literature. It was here that I came across Edgar Allan Poe's early depiction of Antarctica in his short story, *MS. Found in a Bottle* (1833), as well as his essay, *The Philosophy of Composition* (1846), from which I derived the quote, '*the death then of a beautiful woman is unquestionably the most poetical topic in the world, and equally is it beyond doubt that the lips best suited for such topic are those of a bereaved lover.*'

Thank you to my agents, Benython Oldfield, Sharon Galant and Thomasin Chinnery for championing this story from the very beginning. Thank you to everyone at Allen & Unwin for believing in Oli, especially my publisher Kelly Fagan, who quickly became both my friend and my hero. Thank you for believing in this story, even when I didn't. Thank you to my editors Christa Munns, Ali Lavau and Aziza Kuypers. The dream team. Thank you for challenging and supporting me in equal measure.

Thank you to my dear friends Johann Go, Charlie Ford, Kirk Watson, Martin Rosas Carbajal, Ed Chan, Coby Edgar, Isa Frank, Alexander Darby and Yassmin Abdel-Magied for your thorough notes, early criticism and assistance with my research.

Thank you to the Dabalà family in Italy for generously opening their doors to me during my university holidays. It was in your home that I felt safe enough to write my most difficult chapters. Thank you also to Jacquetta Hayes for listening when I first voiced Sea Monsters. Thank you to my sister, Georgia, and my friends in both Australia and England for supporting me on this wild ride. And finally, thank you to my first and last reader, Robbie Mason. This one's for you.